VENGEANCE CALLING

AN AMERICAN MERCENARY THRILLER

JASON KASPER

SEVERN RIVER PUBLISHING

ALSO BY JASON KASPER

American Mercenary Series
Greatest Enemy
Offer of Revenge
Dark Redemption
Vengeance Calling
The Suicide Cartel
Terminal Objective

Shadow Strike Series
The Enemies of My Country
Last Target Standing
Covert Kill
Narco Assassins
Beast Three Six

Spider Heist Thrillers
The Spider Heist
The Sky Thieves
The Manhattan Job
The Fifth Bandit

Standalone Thriller
Her Dark Silence

To find out more about Jason Kasper and his books, visit
severnriverbooks.com/authors/jason-kasper

To Joel

Escendo Evinco

VENGEANCE CALLING

DESTINY

Alea iacta est

-The die is cast

1

January 5, 2009
The Mist Palace
Undisclosed Location, North America

"You've tried to kill me once, David Rivers." A smile twisted the Handler's lips. "I need you to try it again."

His salt-and-pepper hair crowned a gaunt face marred by the crooked skew of his Roman nose. I wondered how it had been broken in the past, then distantly wished I could reproduce the injury before slitting his throat.

Instead I remained immobile, strapped to a chair in the clandestine, mist-soaked North American compound belonging to the international crime leader currently taunting me. I had been shot in three places at the conclusion of a twenty-four-hour bloodbath in the streets and slums of Rio de Janeiro, my humerus shattered by a near point-blank bullet impact, blood-soaked medical dressings freshly applied during the transcontinental flight. I stepped off the plane in North America with a concealed pistol in the splint of my injured arm, fully intent on assassinating the Handler the moment I saw him.

I cleared my throat, unapologetically meeting his eyes. "What makes you think I'll be more successful on my second attempt at ending your life?"

He grinned again, amused, and understandably so—upon approaching him with my hidden pistol, I'd found my friend Ian bound and kneeling at his feet. A single-minded desire for vengeance had driven me toward that meeting; I'd killed many people to get close to the Handler, and would have killed many more.

But never Ian.

He and I were the sole survivors from a mercenary team containing our closest friends, the only family I had. Our combined efforts to avenge them had just been thwarted by an enemy who had known of our plans the entire time. Now Ian was a prisoner, and I was a slave to the Handler's will after he threatened to brutally torture and kill my last living friend if I didn't obey.

The Handler's grin vanished as he straightened to his standing height of a rangy six feet plus. A tremor passed over him, his head shuddering slightly before the serene exterior returned.

"I suspect that an irreplaceable asset in the highest levels of my inner circle is being disloyal." He steepled his fingers beneath his chin, amber eyes focused on me intently. "If I am correct, they are currently plotting my death."

"I can empathize."

His eyes narrowed, but he continued in the same patiently measured cadence of speech. "You will conduct a choreographed assassination attempt in front of this individual. Afterwards, I will give you to them for immediate interrogation and execution. If they betray my order in any way, you will report back to me."

"I imagine the outcome would be relatively obvious," I pointed out, swallowing hard against a growing lump in my throat. "Why would you need me to tell you about it?"

He turned his back, observing the wall behind his desk before addressing me over his shoulder. "The drawback of employing the most brilliant and ruthless of the enlightened caste is their effectiveness at deception—if they execute a conspiracy, it will not be as detectable as yours and Ian's. I must provide the smallest window of opportunity during a routine task for them to betray me. Any greater risks a successful deception, and while I have my own means of verifying the outcome, you are my failsafe."

"And if I survive, and report back?"

The Handler spun to face me, his tone forceful and assured. "I eliminate the traitor. You are granted a conditional pardon, and will be returned to the ranks of my mercenary army."

"If I return to the Outfit, I want to be sent to fight in South America."

"I anticipated you would. My war there is commencing as we speak. If you survive this endeavor, you will immediately be assigned to combat."

I kept my eyes on his, trying to sound undaunted despite a growing feeling of dread spreading within my chest. "What about Ian?"

"In either event, Ian will be safe."

"Then I want him freed, not working for you as a captive."

He leaned down, his expression brimming with fury as he brought his face close to mine and spoke quickly. "Ian will remain employed and under my control. But he will be alive, and your agreement to these terms is the only provision under which he remains so after his *several* attempts on my life." He drew a sharp breath and hissed, "If you do not agree to my terms, your existence—and his— will be reduced to three days of continuous torture, ending when I deliver you both to the chamber—"

"Enough," I interjected, condemning myself to the status of dead man walking in the span of one word. "I'll play your game, as long as Ian lives."

The Handler's expression cooled to its normal state of composure. "Wise decision, David."

"And who among your merry band of criminal misfits do you suspect of having the balls required to betray you? Present company excluded, of course."

The Handler raised a messianic palm to silence me, then turned in a slow, graceful arc toward his desk. He leaned over and lifted a colossal fountain pen wrapped with a gleaming gold oriental dragon carving.

He gracefully carved the pen's nib through an unseen script. Half a minute passed before he paused, capped the pen, and lifted a single piece of paper to the light.

The Handler blew softly across the surface of the sheet with a subtle grin, as if admiring his handiwork, or the order he'd just drafted, or both. Then he laid the paper flat on the desk, folded it into thirds, and slid it into an envelope.

Lifting a blood-red candle from the desk, he lit the wick and let the wax drip onto the envelope flap before impressing a metal stamp onto it for several seconds. As the Handler whisked the sealed envelope up between a thumb and forefinger, he remained stationary as the sudden, neat heel-click of an unseen witness sounded behind me.

I spun my head to the side, taking in the individual who was previously standing behind my chair. He was a runt-sized man in a navy suit, the crown of his head bearing a black yarmulke. He stopped before the desk to accept the envelope.

The Handler ordered, "At the Executive *Karoga* in three weeks' time."

The Jewish man nodded deeply, saying nothing as he spun on his heels and approached me, the sealed envelope clutched in one hand. His face was a balding oval, and oil-spot eyes peered out from behind rimless glasses. The glance he shot me was little more than an appraisal, gathering data as if I were binary code.

Committing my face to memory in the span of half a breath, he turned from me and stepped out of sight, his exit swallowed by the sound of doors closing to my rear.

I looked back to the Handler, opening my mouth to question who he suspected of betraying him. But he silenced me with a wave of one hand as he used the other to hold a phone receiver to his sunken cheek.

He spoke tersely into the phone. "Schedule the full and immediate medical treatment of David Rivers."

2

Three Weeks Later
January 28, 2009

A man's voice said, "David Rivers by direct request. Negative metal, confirmed by 513."

The scrape of metal and a heavy door swinging open were followed by my blacked-out goggles being removed as I blinked to clear my vision. We stood before a room-sized building whose wood siding bore a single door. Two armed guards defended it, wearing plate carriers over civilian clothes and holding compact M4 assault rifles. A black forest surrounded us, and buildings were only visible in glimpses between trees. The trails weaving through the forest were illuminated by dim solar lighting, causing the interlocking treetops to appear phantasmal amid a billowing ceiling of fog. A snowless winter, damp and foggy, punctuated by glimpses of chain link fence and barbed wire lurking in whispers among the forest.

I was no longer required to wear handcuffs within the Mist Palace, a gracious concession given that my left arm was now pinned to my side by a black sling against a wedge of foam, my left hand holding a red rubber squeeze ball for rehabilitation. My fractured humerus had been surgically fixed by titanium plates, and my other two muscle wounds were likewise treated as a complimentary medical service in exchange for getting shot three times for the Organization in Brazil. Healthcare within the Handler's international crime syndicate was effective and immediate...but it came at a much greater cost, one that I was about to pay in full.

Beside me, Ishway slid my blacked-out goggles into his overcoat pocket as naturally as if he were putting away a cigarette case.

Between his height, carved Asian features, and the long hair swept back into a low bun, there was nothing particularly commanding about Ishway's appearance. Yet in the weeks since he escorted me off the return flight from Rio and into the confrontation that would change the tide of my destiny—and Ian's—I increasingly wondered about Ishway's exact role in the Organization. Always dressed head to toe in lavish business attire, he glided through the halls in sartorial aplomb, usually toting a leather-bound ledger and always to the great deference of the guard force.

Ishway said, "Enjoy, Mr. Rivers. I will transport you back to your room upon the conclusion of dinner."

"You're not among the anointed ones dining here tonight?"

"I'm afraid not."

"That's a shame," I quipped, looking around to see that two more members of the guard force had trailed me and now stood patiently waiting for Ishway's order to depart. They were clad with the same plate carriers and assault rifles as the guards on duty outside the building, one of whom now held open the lone door for me.

What was all this security for, in the end? The compound was very remote, with only a few select pilots knowing the exact coordinates to reach the airfield. Yet visitors like myself were still required to wear blacked-out goggles when escorted through the Handler's inner layers of security. What kind of attack could they possibly be expecting?

I returned my gaze to Ishway's unsettlingly tranquil face.

"Well," I concluded, "I'll be breathlessly awaiting our next reunion, Ishway."

Without waiting for a response, I strode past the guards and into the building, finding myself in a large cooking and dining area.

In place of a roof was an elevated overhang designed to prevent surveillance from above. While it was close to freezing outside, free-standing air heaters around the long dining table generated a cozy humming sound and a comfortable warmth in a room dominated by the smell of extravagantly seasoned food.

Four guards maintained their stoic vigil in the corners, hands clutching silenced submachine guns, automatic pistols holstered on their waists. They were clean-cut, freshly shaven, and armed for precision shooting inside a room: the Secret Service minus any need for professional discretion. Their eyes were fixed on me with thinly veiled contempt, though they were probably equally irritated by any newcomer who disrupted their established security routine.

But within the next few minutes, both the face and name of David Rivers would be burned into their psyche for the rest of their careers.

One wall of the room held a row of charcoal-burning stoves being serviced by an older man who turned as I entered. The Handler's personal bodyguard stood behind the head of the table, where three other men were already seated: the Handler, a fashionably handsome man with silver hair I'd never seen before, and the slight man in the yarmulke.

My eyes faltered on the Jewish man before I forced my gaze to the head of the table, where the Handler was watching me. The amber glint of his eyes was clear even from across the room, his gaze that of a wolf languidly watching prey because it knew the rest of the pack was already in place for the kill.

"Our guest of honor," the Handler said, wielding a hand to the seat beside him. "Please, join us."

I rounded the dining table toward them. The silver-haired man stood and offered his hand. He was easily in his sixties, with movie-star looks, a stylish, perfectly combed haircut, and an easy, broad smile revealing neat rows of white teeth. The top few buttons of his dress shirt were casually undone, a pitch-perfect Hollywood vision in all ways except one: the upper left side of his face was marred by what appeared to be claw marks streaking downward from forehead to cheekbone, narrowly missing the intervening eye.

He shook my hand briskly as he spoke with a gruff Boston accent. "Watts. Chief Vicar of Defense. Well done in Rio, David." He was grinning broadly, facial scars contorted with genuine enthusiasm—he truly didn't know the reason for my attendance this evening, I decided. I briefly pondered the title of "vicar," a word used by religious officials, not governments. "How're you recovering from your injuries?"

"Quite well." I nodded to the red squeeze ball held limply in my left hand. "This sling is a great conversation starter, but I'm a little disappointed the Organization doesn't have a Purple Heart equivalent. Would've gone great with my vanity plate, probably save me a few speeding tickets."

"Medals are overrated, any vet will tell you that—but money? That's fair remuneration, much more suited for our line of work." Watts didn't break eye contact to investigate the sling on my arm until our handshake was complete, and then he twisted his facial scar toward the man in the yarmulke, who remained seated. "Allow me to introduce our Chief Vicar of Intelligence, Yosef."

The Jewish man remained completely immobile save the slightest hint of a nod. Short, thin, nearly a dwarf, he was again clad in a resplendent navy suit and said nothing. He didn't need to—he and I shared an understanding independent of everyone in the room other than the Handler himself.

"No need to get up," I said to Yosef. "The pleasure's all mine."

Watts gave a scoff of amusement. "Don't take it personally, David. He's a man of few words."

"Must be a real hit at parties."

"That's what our chef is for. David, meet Omari."

The portly chef intercepted the introduction, wiping a hand on his apron and extending it to shake mine eagerly. While his dark skin and thick black mustache gave him the appearance of an Indian, he spoke with an African accent.

"Omari. Your chef for this evening."

Watts added, "He also holds a minor position in the executive staff."

"Details." Omari dismissed Watts's words with a wave of his hand. "As Chief Vicar of Finance, I am replaceable. As *karoga* chef, I am one-of-a-kind. Perhaps in all of North America. You are about to dine like you've never dined before, my friend."

The Handler picked up an elegant bottle of scotch from the table. "Now that our guest of honor is here, we shall start the *karoga*."

Pulling out the cork, he dropped it before crushing it with the heel of his shoe. "This means we will finish the bottle, David. The first drink is reserved for those lost on the journey, that they might nonetheless join us here."

He tipped the bottle downward with the toast, "For the earth," and a shot of scotch splattered against the concrete floor. Then he took a sip before handing the bottle to Watts. I was next, accepting the sculpted glass bottle and appraising the label: *Macallan 1926.*

"Hope you didn't go to all this trouble for me," I offered. "My astonishment can be bought for a lot less than what this bottle probably cost."

Watts procured a pack of cigarettes from his pocket, drawing one and tossing the rest onto the table. "Not anymore, David. You could have a Porsche 911 for the price of that bottle."

He lit his smoke as I took a sip, tasting the peaty musk of scotch before it transitioned into a bouquet of dried fruit and licorice. The residue turned to a rich cedar in my mouth before whisking away altogether.

"God*damn*." I winced. "I'd take this bottle over the car."

Omari grunted in approval and reached for the bottle, but I pulled it away from him. "Apologies, Omari—I caught a wicked case of mono in Brazil. Probably best I hang onto this scotch and you guys open a new one."

He snatched the bottle from me. "Fuck that. Nothing is sacred at a *karoga*, sickness or no. We drink, we talk shit, we smoke cigarettes. Nothing is forbidden to discuss, no one may get offended. This is why no women are allowed."

"Until Parvaneh assumes the throne," Watts pointed out.

Omari took a swig, mustache spreading as he momentarily cringed before passing the bottle to Yosef. "Until that day."

I almost winced at the mention of the Handler's daughter. In Rio I had joined Parvaneh's delegation, fought to defend her when we came under attack, and had ultimately taken three bullets to save her life. We'd felt the mutual pangs of romance—until she learned that I was an assassin infiltrating the Organization with the sole purpose of killing her father.

Now, even under the current circumstances, and even with the events in Rio setting off a full-fledged war between criminal networks, I couldn't bear the thought of Parvaneh's electric green eyes burning into me.

"What does *karoga* mean?" I asked, sweeping my thoughts aside as I watched Yosef drink. His inscrutable eyes darted around the table as he swallowed and wordlessly passed the bottle to the Handler.

Omari turned his pot belly back to a tall steel pot simmering on an open charcoal flame and stirred the contents with a long wooden spoon. "My ancestors were laborers in India when the British began building the Kenya-Uganda Railway. The call went out for workers, and my ancestors boarded *dowlas*—small fishing boats—bringing only what they could carry on their person. They crossed the Indian Ocean in search of a better life— and those of them that survived the voyage became laborers on the railroad."

"And learned to drink like Kenyans," Watts added, passing the bottle to me for a second round.

I raised the bottle to my lips, only letting enough scotch enter my mouth to make the sip look convincing. My alcohol tolerance was both immense and hard-earned, but I'd need every possible iota of speed for what I was about to do.

Omari looked over his shoulder, continuing, "...this is how my ancestors dined—after a long day of building the railroad, getting eaten by lions, and dying of malaria, they would assemble around huge cooking pots with whatever food and spices they could gather. *Karoga* means 'stir' in Swahili, and that is what these meals become—'The Stir,' because every family would take turns cooking. It is not Indian, not Kenyan—it is a unique merger, you would say."

The food smelled delicious, an intoxicating blend of smoky cumin, fresh ginger, and sautéed onions over roasting chicken. Watts's and Yosef's cigarette smoke cut through the scent of food as the Handler reached for the pack of cigarettes while addressing me.

"We reserve the Executive *Karoga* for events demanding celebration. Saving my daughter and the heir to this dynasty qualifies."

Watts blew a stream of smoke toward the roof overhang, the dissipating cloud of silver matching the color of his hair. "Parvaneh's bodyguard spoke very highly of your valor in Rio."

"Her bodyguard commended me?"

"You sound surprised." He offered me a cigarette, which I declined with a wave of my hand.

"Please, Watts, not until I'm accustomed to the taste of scotch that costs more per shot than any bottle I've ever bought in my life. And yes, I'm surprised—her bodyguard seemed about as fond of me as Yosef does. How's the war in Brazil going, anyway?"

"Brazil?" he scoffed, handing the cigarettes to Yosef. "Try half of South America. We've been operating in Bolivia, Venezuela, Colombia...the group that tried to kill Parvaneh has a wide reach."

"I wasn't part of the Outfit for long, but I don't recall them being big enough to handle that kind of action. You guys have a reserve force, or what?"

"Hell no. We're just using local mercenaries for most of the grunt work, led and equipped by Outfit advisors. Unilateral Outfit strike teams are reserved for high-profile targets, anyone higher up in the organization. We've been slicing and dicing their soldiers, but the executive staff are slippery sons of bitches. They've got a sophisticated evasion network, as well they should—they've been doing it long enough. Hiding from the government, hiding from cartel hitters. Hell, you saw how protective they were of their leader when you met with him in Brazil, am I right, David?"

I nodded distantly, recalling how Parvaneh's delegation had been stripped of location trackers; taken on a route to lose all surveillance, complete with decoy vehicles; and then delivered to a high-rise meeting that the organization's top leader departed via helicopter before we were allowed to return to our people.

And that was before he'd tried to have us all killed.

"They were cautious, yes," I said. "I guess they'd need to be, given who they were crossing." I looked around to see that the bodyguards hadn't moved an inch, just shifted their weight from one foot to the other with a metronome-like regularity reserved for men who'd spent a majority of their adult lives pretending to be statues. Yosef slowly pulled a cigarette from the pack, his eyes never leaving my face.

"Goddamn right," Watts said between drags. "I don't mean that we've never lost a war—we haven't, but that's not my point. What I'm saying is we've never failed to run down every high-profile individual associated with the opposition..."

Turning my head, I saw the Handler's personal bodyguard standing a few paces behind us, his hands folded neatly over his waist. I had previously nicknamed him Racegun due to the modified pistol he carried, and while he was standing casually I knew his reflexes exceeded anyone else's in the room.

Across the table from me, Yosef lit his cigarette. He lowered his hand, ember tilted upward to pour a thin trail of smoke to the roof, his enigmatic face remaining completely expressionless even though he knew what I was about to do.

Watts was still speaking. "...once somebody crosses the Organization, their lifespan drops to thirty days or less in most cases. If someone's really got unlimited resources at their disposal, they might make it a year. But we always get our man—"

He fell silent as Racegun murmured "Copy" into his shirt cuff and stepped forward to touch the Handler's shoulder, whispering something in his ear.

The Handler lowered his cigarette and listened intently, lips curling in consideration as the rest of us sat in rapt attention. Finally his head bobbed in a slight nod. "Very well. Bring it to me."

Racegun stepped back and swung an index finger toward the single door.

The bodyguard manning the entrance announced, "Sir, your message."

He opened the door and a curvy female entered, her red hair pulled back into a ponytail.

I recognized her at once as Sage, the lone woman who first delivered me to the Mist Palace via the Handler's private jet. Our cryptic in-flight conversation had left me wondering who she was, but virtually all memory of her had been erased from my mind in the wake of what happened in Brazil days later.

Until now, as she entered the Executive *Karoga*, which I had been admitted to for one reason alone.

Her lithe beauty struck me as she advanced toward the Handler, a folded piece of paper in her hand swinging alongside her rounded hip.

Omari and Watts turned their heads to watch her, and who could blame them? Even Yosef's silent gaze was turned toward the display of fiery grace unexpectedly descending upon the *karoga*. Sage's face registered a slight look of surprise at my presence, and we locked eyes for a split second as the undertow of adrenaline in my bloodstream surged into an all-encompassing wave.

As the Handler's glimmering eyes twitched up at Sage amid a puff of exhaled cigarette smoke, I took a sharp breath. Grabbing the steak knife beside my plate in an icepick grip, I swung it toward the Handler's jugular in one desperate movement—a fraction of a second meant the difference between slaying my greatest enemy and tumbling into a far different fate.

The jagged point was inches from carving its way through the Handler's neck before Racegun's powerful grip intercepted my arm, stopping it mid-swing and smashing my hand against the table.

"*DOWN!*" Racegun shouted, and what happened next told me everything I needed to know about the Handler's security protocol.

Before Racegun could finish torqueing my right hand behind my back, the other four bodyguards in the room had their submachine guns aimed at Watts, Omari, Yosef, and Sage. I heard the slap of palms against the table as the Handler's high council assumed prostrate positions of total submission, heads hanging low over their plates lest they be shot.

Sage stood completely still, her folded paper fluttering to the floor as she held her hands up, eyes turned downward in surrender.

Racegun spun me out of my chair and threw me against the wall, the jarring impact against my left arm making my vision go bleary with exploding tears of intense pain. One of the other bodyguards took physical control of me as Racegun grabbed the Handler, jerking him to his feet and racing him toward the door being pulled open by the attending guard.

Less than ten seconds after I reached for my knife, the Handler was evacuated. Every bodyguard followed his royal presence out the door save the one holding me, who shortly thereafter decided to remove me as an immediate threat by delivering a crushing knockout blow to my temple.

3

My right wrist was chained to the table in front of me. The spartan room was brightly lit, with two chairs bolted to the floor on either side of the table. I sat in one of them, facing a windowless metal door. A mirror covered one wall, and I briefly wondered who was watching from the other side. The black orbs of ceiling-mounted surveillance cameras watched me coldly, indifferent to my upcoming interrogation and execution.

My legitimate attempt to kill the Handler upon returning from Rio had been witnessed only by Ian, Parvaneh, and a small security detail in the garden of the Mist Palace. But at the *karoga* a few hours earlier, I'd swung a knife at the Handler's throat in full view of his entire executive staff, and only Yosef and the Handler knew it had been a planned charade. There was no going back now, no fallback ploy. I was completely committed to whatever—and whoever—walked through that door. The Handler refused to tell me whom he suspected, but judging by his bizarre plan and the grave tone with which he ordered it into existence, it was someone worthy of his concern.

I felt confident the offending party was Watts, the silver-haired Boston movie star serving as the Handler's Chief Vicar of Defense. He seemed the best bet by far. Omari, the *karoga* chef and finance chief, had been too jovial, too upbeat, to harbor any dark conspiratorial notions. And Yosef, having personally accepted the order as Chief Vicar of Intelligence, was beyond suspicion.

I finally heard a bolt click within the door, and I watched it expectantly, waiting for it to open. At last, the hinges creaked and I saw a solitary figure standing in the gap.

For the second time since entering the *karoga*, I was taken aback by who I saw—and for the same reason.

Sage's vibrant red hair was now pulled back into a smart ponytail, and her professional attire modestly covered her shapely form. We watched each other in silence for a moment before she spoke.

"Good evening, Mr. Rivers."

Under different circumstances I would have laughed at the sight of her. The Handler controlled a small army of cutthroat mercenaries, bodyguards, and psychopathic deviants, yet he was concerned about the one employee who looked like an off-duty swimsuit model.

"Good evening, Sage." I lifted my right hand helplessly against the chain. "I always seem to be a captive audience when you're around."

Her face remained cold as she slid into the seat across from me before opening a small notebook and jotting something down. "I am here to investigate why you attempted to assassinate the One. You can tell me of your own free will, or we can resort to more drastic—"

"Relax, Sage. No need for theatrics."

She leaned closer, lips parting for a second of silence before she managed, "Theatrics?"

"Look, I've got no living friends that I can betray by telling you the truth, so let's get this over with. We both know how this is going to end for me."

Although her eyes remained flat, I sensed she was concealing some emotion I couldn't discern—was it approval, even delight?

"Very well. I have been tasked with composing a report on the incident that occurred at the Executive *Karoga* earlier this evening. So start with why you attempted to kill the One. From the beginning, please."

I leaned back in my chair, leaving my handcuffed wrist atop the table. Sage began scrawling in the notebook as a formality—the whole room was doubtless wired for audio coverage. I began, "Short version? I was medically discharged from the Army last year. I had a score to settle with a man named Peter McAlister, and I murdered him in his home. Later that night three men apprehended me—"

"Their names?"

"I knew them as Boss, Matz, and Ophie."

She tilted her head. "Criminals?"

"Yes." I found myself nodding distantly, recalling their faces, voices, mannerisms. "What was left of a paramilitary team that conducted operations for the Handler. They recruited me to work with them."

"In what capacity?"

Releasing a sigh, I replied, "As an assassin."

"I need a list of targets," she said at once. "Everyone you killed or are aware of them killing."

"My first job was against a business executive named Saamir, at his high rise in Chicago last summer. Then I watched the team torture and execute a man named Luka for killing one of their previous teammates, and together we wiped out a safe house full of guards to eliminate a primary target and gain intelligence to target the Five Heads."

"Tell me about the Five Heads."

"To my knowledge, they were the US-based opposition to the Handler. He got them together for a negotiation via teleconference, and when they were united he sent my team to conduct a decapitation strike. Matz's sister" —my voice faltered here—"was named Karma. She was one of the getaway drivers. I was in love with her. When our strike against the Five Heads was successful, the Handler had our entire team wiped out. I was the only survivor."

I watched her face for surprise or contrition, seeing neither. Instead she made a notation that ended with her spinning the pen toward me. "And how does the only survivor end up seated next to the One at the Executive *Karoga*?"

A wave of nausea hit me as I prepared to recount a journey that had ended in failure on every conceivable metric. "I was contacted by a man who gave me an offer of revenge. He had me recruited by the Handler's personal mercenary unit."

"The Outfit."

"Yes. I earned admission last year."

She stopped writing abruptly. "Who contacted you?"

"I don't know his name, or how he found me. I only met him once. Heavyset Indian man. All he said was that he'd have the Outfit call me to enter their selection process. Told me that was the only way I could get close to the Handler if I wanted to kill him, which I do. My first Outfit mission was in Somalia in December. I'd just returned when you picked me up to meet the Handler."

She seemed satisfied with my responses thus far, as she should—my story was almost the complete truth. I only left out the fact that Ian survived with me and had initiated my contact with the Indian. This was safe territory for me to lie. The Handler's people would support the redaction as part of my current mole hunt.

Sage set her pen down beside the open notebook. "After I delivered you to the Mist Palace upon your return from Somalia, what occurred at your first meeting with the One?"

"The Handler assigned me to the protective detail of his daughter, Parvaneh, for the upcoming negotiations in Rio de Janeiro."

"Why would he assign a new Outfit operator to such a critical role?"

I actually guffawed. "Because he's a lunatic." She seemed irritated by this response. "He believed a prophecy from a woman in Somalia stating that I'd save his daughter's life."

A cool smile of assurance from Sage. "To my understanding, you *did* save his daughter's life."

"Blind luck," I shot back. "But it bought me an honorary seat at the Executive *Karoga*, so tonight I did my best to paint that room with his arterial spray."

She plucked her pen from the table and made a final annotation before closing her notebook. "I'll submit my report to the Intelligence Directorate. They'll confirm or deny your statement."

"How about a bottle of Woodford Reserve while I wait? Last meal and all that."

She suppressed a grin, unsure exactly what to make of me.

"I'll be back, Mr. Rivers."

With that, she rose and left the room.

* * *

The morning of my execution was an unseasonably warm winter day. As I walked blindly forward in blacked-out goggles, the mild air against the exposed skin of my face and hands felt almost like spring.

I was led into the back of a truck or van, felt the creaking shift of the floor beneath me before the handcuff on my right wrist was transferred to a fixed anchor point.

Sage spoke quietly, matter-of-factly. "Just a short ride, and it will all be over. Are you going to remain quiet, or should I give you the injection now?"

"If I've got a curvy redhead chaining me up, I'll take the good with the bad. I won't give you any trouble."

"They all say that."

"Then let's hold off on the injection while I think of something original."

She exited the back, and I heard a hatch close and lock behind me. We began driving, rumbling along a dirt road before coming to a stop. A chain link gate rattled open to our front and we began moving again, and I heard it clang shut behind us before a second gate opened. The path transitioned from smooth dirt to rough trail with a series of increasingly jarring bumps as we headed away from the Mist Palace to places unknown.

After what felt like an hour, the truck braked sharply.

I heard the driver's door open and slam shut, followed by the entrance to my compartment being unlocked and thumping footsteps as someone entered. My goggles were stripped away, and I could finally take in my surroundings.

I was in the back of a covered truck, and Sage was now beside me, wearing an expression of frantic urgency.

"Do exactly as I say." She unlocked my wrist cuff, leaving it to dangle from the anchor point. "If you don't, we're both dead."

"Both of us?"

"Get out of the truck. Hurry."

I stepped onto a dirt and rock path whose serpentine twists took it through a craggy forest floor, sunlight filtering dimly through a roof of pine trees rising high above us. Sage was hunched in the flatbed, flipping the rubber floor mat out of the truck toward me. Then she ran her fingers under the bench until I heard the click of a hidden latch and a panel comprising most of the truck bed shifted upward.

She pulled it off, and a man sat up from a false bottom in the truck.

He squinted as he adjusted to the sudden change in his surroundings, pulling himself out of the compartment with his right arm only—and when I saw why, a chill of fear ran up my spine.

His left arm was hidden in a black sling, hand loosely clutching a red rubber ball identical to the one I held. Likewise, he was dressed in the same prisoner jumpsuit that I was, and as he took in my features at a glance, his face transformed into a solemn mask of understanding. I felt my mouth hanging open, my mind grinding to a state of shock.

His face mirrored mine as much as his arm sling and clothes—iridescent green eyes, short, dark blond hair—even his nose and cheekbones bore more than a passing similarity.

Sage addressed him firmly. "Quickly, Nikolai."

He nodded and climbed out of the truck as I nearly yelled at Sage, "Stop, you fucking idiot!"

"What do you mean, *stop*? I'm saving your life."

"The Handler is testing you—you have to kill me, or my friend dies."

"I know it's a test. I've known for weeks. Obey the Handler, and Ian spends his life a slave. Obey me, and Ian will be freed."

"You can't fool the Handler, he knows everything—"

"If I didn't know every aspect of his test, we wouldn't be speaking right now." Turning now to Nikolai, who stepped shakily toward the forest, she said, "Be strong. Otherwise, your family gets nothing."

He gave her a weak, forced smile. "Thank you."

I tried to place his Eastern European accent. Polish? Hungarian?

He spun in place, barely completing his turn away from us before Sage shot him.

A faint puff on the back of his head and a momentary eruption of crimson as he crumpled to the damp forest floor. The red rubber ball sprang free from his hand, bouncing off a moss-covered stone before disappearing amid a bed of ferns.

I felt frozen in place, unable to comprehend the speed with which my circumstances had spun 180 degrees, as the sound of approaching vehicles sliced through the forest.

Sage leveled her cool gray eyes at me.

"Get in the compartment, Mr. Rivers. You've got ten seconds to decide or we're both dead."

If I rebelled against her plan, she would likely kill me. And if she didn't, the Handler just as easily could—he was a known quantity of manipulation and evil against the mystery surrounding this woman and her intentions. It was a spin of the roulette wheel, and in the urgency of that moment I had to gamble with both my life and Ian's.

Without another thought, I spun and darted into the truck bed. My adrenaline was through the roof, images of Ian and the Handler racing through my mind as I slid into the coffin-sized slot in the floor and she pulled the cover back into place over me. I heard the thump of the floor mat being situated to hide the compartment, then a rustled thumping over me that I realized was her rolling Nikolai's body into the bed before the back door slammed shut. I was encapsulated amid the smell of Nikolai's sweat and fear permeating the false bottom compartment while my heart felt like it was going to explode out of my chest.

The truck engine growled to life and we rolled forward again, proceeding for less than a minute before stopping abruptly.

"Kill the engine," a man's voice commanded, and our truck went silent.

Sage shouted, "What's the meaning of this?"

"Is your prisoner in the back?"

"Of course he is."

"What was the gunshot we just heard?"

"I heard a thumping sound in the back. I stopped the truck, unlocked it, and saw that the prisoner had picked his handcuff and was trying to force open the cargo door. He tried to escape, and I shot him. So what?"

"Open the back."

"This is a routine drop—"

"You know better than to question protocol. Open it, or I'm taking you into custody."

I heard the back door unlock and swing open.

20

"Satisfied?" Sage asked. "Now if you'll allow, I have a transfer to make."

"You're not going anywhere." A pause before he continued, "This is Alpha one-five. Send the biometrics team to link up with me on Route Candace, five hundred meters south of checkpoint Charlie two-three."

"Copy, on the way."

"Biometrics team?" Sage questioned, sounding offended. "What is going on?"

"All you need to know is that our orders come from the One."

I heard another vehicle approach and stop, then the sound of people dismounting and climbing into the back of the truck. New voices now, muted and hollow as I felt their weight shifting on the floor above me.

"Make sure you photodocument everything."

"Got it. Start with known injuries."

"Scarring on right shoulder, left deltoid, and left bicep all consistent with gunshot wounds within the past four weeks."

"I confirm. Proceed to surgical identifier."

"There's a longitudinal scar extending midline of the posterior arm, from just inferior to the acromion process down to the olecranon fossa. Scar has red appearance, edges slightly raised. I'd say it's two to three weeks old, with stitches removed sometime in the past seventy-two hours."

"Agreed. Scar is consistent with posterior humeral shaft open reduction and internal fixation procedure undergone by subject. Outfit identifiers?"

"Raised circular scarring on left bicep and between two left ribs, likely cigarette burns."

"Consistent with injuries sustained by subject during Outfit Selection Round 2-2009. Let's move on to the obvious injury."

"There's a mosaic fracture to the skull...clean edge of the wound is flat and round, interior edge of skull has conchoidal beveling. Massive trauma to brain area and sinus canal, and upper dental plate is cracked."

"Positive infrared pattern consistent with gunshot residue, pattern of dispersal approximately six inches, estimate muzzle to target distance of one and a half feet. Sodium rhodizonate confirms presence of lead. All observable trauma consistent with gunshot wound, where bullet entered the back of the skull and exited through the face. Agreed?"

"Without a doubt."

"Let's proceed to live-scan."

A long pause.

"Friction ridge analysis of left thumb and index consistent with points of identification. Checking right thumb and index...ridge ending, bifurcation, delta, core...all consistent with subject."

"Rapid blood typing result consistent with A Positive."

"Retinal scan and bite pattern are both inconclusive due to damage from probable gunshot wound. But the filling in right deciduous mandibular second molar is consistent with work from subject's known dental record. So that's it."

"That's it? You're done?"

"Buccal swab of skin cells in the mouth isn't an instant result, but we'll run it to the lab and confirm or deny DNA profile within a few hours. Pending that result, everything checks out with our subject."

"You're ready to confirm?"

"Yes. I confirm positive identification of David Clayton Rivers, Outfit Member Number 296."

"All right. Take your team back to the house."

Sage's voice now, sounding smug. "Satisfied?"

"Continue with your transfer. Complete a full written report upon your return."

"I will."

The sound of vehicles pulling away, and then my truck rumbled forward once more.

This leg of the journey lasted another hour, my body shifting forward and back in the tight confines of the false bottom compartment. When the truck stopped again, I heard the murmur of indistinguishable words. The engine was left running as Sage recovered me from the compartment, and I climbed out past Nikolai's corpse, now slumped in a pile to one side of the truck.

She led me into the trees as the truck pulled forward down the trail, piloted by an unseen driver.

I spoke quietly as I followed her into the forest. "How did you install a false bottom in one of the Handler's vehicles?"

"Mr. Rivers, the false bottom wasn't a clandestine installment. The entire vehicle was an identical replica, and one procured at great expense."

"All that trouble just to save me?"

"All that trouble," she agreed, "just to save you."

Our foot trail led to a blanket of camouflage netting draped over a waist-height shape.

I asked, "Don't think that I'm not grateful, but...why?"

She pulled off the camouflage netting to reveal a flat black all-terrain vehicle. The ATV's hood and bumper were laden with black fuel cans covered by custom-fitted cargo bags with bulging zippered pouches. The vehicle was rigged for expeditionary use, the state of its knobby tires telling me this thing had spent many hours threading through the mountain trails of our surroundings.

She unzipped one of the cargo pouches, withdrawing an olive GORE-TEX cold weather coat and handing it to me. I slid my right arm into the sleeve and pulled the left side over my sling as she straddled the ATV and looked back at me.

"Get on, Mr. Rivers."

I straddled the seat behind her, threading my right arm around her tight stomach.

She fired the engine, and the ATV whirred to life with a muted growl. Whether it had a custom engine, custom exhaust, or both, it was surreally quiet for an all-terrain vehicle—she only had to slightly raise her voice over the idling engine for me to hear her say, "The ride will be rough."

"Why is this turning me on?"

"Don't be a smartass. It's going to be murder on your injured arm."

"Quicker recovery time than getting shot in the head. Where are we?"

"Somewhere in the Cascades of British Columbia. He has GPS jammers covering a wide swath around the Mist Palace, so that's about as specific as I can get."

"Then where are we going?"

"You'll find out in a couple hours."

Then she raced us forward along an ill-defined, muddy path that plunged through a stream before climbing a rocky slope on the far side of the ravine. The pain in my injured arm was nauseating, every bump in the trail tenderizing my flesh. Deeper we raced into a dark forest, the sun's foggy rays dimming with each passing minute. Sage negotiated the winding trail with expertly timed bursts of acceleration and braking, the ATV moving as quickly as the ground conditions allowed.

Finally she stopped the ATV, giving me a merciful reprieve to take long, slow breaths in an attempt to steady the brutal pain of my recent surgical repair.

She killed the engine, exposing a thumping cadence of sunset birdcalls that permeated the forest as she asked, "How's your arm doing?"

"I'm starting to wish you had killed me." I grimaced.

"Make no mistake, Mr. Rivers—I did kill you." She unzipped a cargo pouch draped behind the handlebars, retrieving a night vision device and pulling the head mount over her red hair. While tightening its straps, she continued, "And it's just a matter of time before the Handler finds a way to make my death appear incidental. Think of your return from Somalia. Have you wondered why he told the Outfit he'd be arriving on the jet when it was just me? It was to draw out assassins—he is well aware there are several of them working at the Outfit. If that plane got blown up by a rocket, I'd be killed in the process. As would the assassins. Believe me when I say the Handler is not above sending me to death in the line of duty, much less you."

"I get that, but why not just kill you if he suspects you're working against him?"

"I'm not expendable."

"Everyone's expendable."

She started the engine and said, "Speak for yourself, Mr. Rivers," before she pulled forward again.

My mind reeled at this last detail stacked upon the others. In the short time since I'd left the Mist Palace, I'd gotten a behind-the-scenes view of an identical replica truck with a false bottom, a willing victim to serve as my body double who had apparently undergone physical modifications to replicate my scars, and a heavily customized ATV outfitted for stealthy long-range use.

Taken with Sage's apparent knowledge of the Handler's entire plan to entrap her, complete with a fully outfitted biometrics team and the digital records swap required to trick them, I was no closer to understanding who she was or what her plan entailed, but I was increasingly certain that Sage wasn't running an amateur operation.

The wilderness around us faded to inky blackness as the temperature plummeted. From the speed with which she carved our ATV through the darkness, I could tell she wasn't relying on ambient light alone—the vehicle must have been equipped with an infrared headlight, allowing Sage to see the trail under night vision almost as clearly as if it were daytime.

When she finally brought the ATV to a stop again, she killed the engine and activated the beam of a red flashlight as we dismounted.

"This way," she ordered.

Her flashlight's crimson glow illuminated weathered wooden stairs that we climbed to a door. I followed her carefully into a building, and she activated a camping lantern within.

The harsh white light illuminated the interior of an ancient cabin. One corner was stacked high with crates of field rations, bottled water, and miscellaneous supplies like toilet paper, shower wipes, first aid kits, and batteries. The other corner contained a cold weather sleeping bag, clothing ranging from thermal underwear to fleece jackets, and a jumble of color-coded elastic bands piled on top of a white binder.

Sage oriented me quickly, her voice crisp and businesslike. "These are your materials and instructions for completing physical therapy for your arm. I'm going to need you at full strength. There's a small bedroom and woodstove in the back, and as many books as I could transport up here. You'll find an outhouse behind the cabin, along with plenty of firewood and an ax if you need to chop more, but don't create smoke during the day if the mist has lifted."

I glanced around the cabin, my gaze settling on her. "Why'd the Handler pick Canada, of all places?"

"He's got locations all over the world," she explained. "All isolated, all developed just enough to be reinforced or occupied with people when he needs full-purpose functionality."

"And the Mist Palace?"

"Built at the site of an abandoned mining community from the Cariboo Gold Rush. Mid-1800s. A decade ago it was nothing more than an old settlement in ruins, with just enough overgrown trails in its vicinity to facilitate transit." Sage hesitated, then continued, "It happened to be the nearest residence when he almost died of a botched assassination last September."

I was still in exile then—that must have been Ian's failed attempt.

Brushing the thought aside, I said, "Who are you, Sage, and why are you not expendable?"

"I'm a wet woman, Mr. Rivers."

"An assassin?"

Sage shook her head. "Not just an assassin. I possess the tradecraft to gain access to some very important people, the artistry of seduction to lure them into private settings, and the lethality required to kill them and escape." She didn't seem embarrassed, relaying her skill sets with the sober diction of a professional resume. A tone of pride colored her voice when she continued, "One or two of these traits isn't hard to find. The combination of all three is next to impossible. And I've got an impeccable service record."

I considered this information before countering, "But how have you been able to plot against—"

"I share a trait held by every high-ranking double agent of the last eighty years: I can lie to polygraphs without detection. He has no proof that I'm disloyal, and to kill me on a whim would disenfranchise an organization kept in power through assassination attempts and conspiracies. No sitting Handler wants to taunt that."

"What about the other three conspirators who helped free me?"

At this, her long eyelashes fluttered in amusement. "Who said there were three?"

"One who delivered the ATV to you and took over your execution truck, and one who fed you the information about the Handler's test in advance. You would've needed both to know where to stage my death—just far enough from the Handler's inspectors to give you time for the switch, just close enough that your lateness wouldn't have been suspicious."

"That's only two."

"I'm assuming neither of those participants had the hacking skills required to alter the biometric records in my Outfit file."

"Interesting theory." She shrugged noncommittally. "I have no comment on the matter, Mr. Rivers."

I corrected her in a reassuring tone. "Now, now, Sage—you faked my death, kidnapped me, and are dumping me in a remote cabin. You've earned the right to call me David." Then I nodded toward the supplies. "So where are you hiding the alcohol, Sage?"

"I need you sober. And please don't try to leave. There's no way in or out except ATV, no civilization within hiking distance, and enough bears and wolves that you'd get killed if you tried."

I turned my palms upward in frustration. "So what am I supposed to do?"

"Make sure your arm is fully recovered." She nodded toward my sling. "You're going to need it. Wait for my return and—"

"Who was Nikolai?"

She stopped abruptly.

"A willing participant," she answered at last, "and one well-compensated for his role."

"You mean his life."

"In this case, the two are one and the same. You have some reservations about benefitting from his sacrifice?"

"Enough reservations to wonder why you're going through all this just to save me."

"Then I'll be blunt." She faced me, staring into my eyes amid the dim light of the camping lantern. "I need someone who is willing to die, can kill wantonly, and is thought to be dead." She took a deep breath and let it out slowly. "Like my own job qualifications, finding someone with one or two of these isn't a difficult task. But the combination of all three is next to impossible."

I felt my throat closing. "And you need me to do what, exactly?"

"I saw it in your eyes the day I picked you up at the Complex: the desire for vengeance, the despair when you realized he wasn't on the plane. Do as I say, David, and you'll finally get your chance."

"My chance for what?" I asked.

"To kill the Handler."

I watched her blankly as she continued, "I'll be back for you in a month or so."

"A month *or so*? What if a truck hits you before then? Who else knows I'm here?"

Sage smiled grimly, saying nothing.

Then she turned and hurried down the stairs, and the ATV fired up and pulled away. The sound of its engine fading into the night was soon replaced by the warbling cry of wolves howling in the darkness all around me.

SOLITUDE

Hic sunt dracones

-Here there are dragons

4

February 1, 2009

At daybreak, I stood in the cabin doorway, preparing to exit for the first time.

Sunrise revealed the cabin to be tiny and dilapidated, scarcely bigger in square footage than an average bedroom or two. A single tin chimney extended upward from moldy wooden roof planks, and a porch outcropping was held up by shaky boughs. The windows were thin panes of splotched glass that provided no more reprieve from the outside temperature than the frail walls. At best, the cabin would block wind and rain, but little else.

Just outside the door, I found the ax that Sage had mentioned. It was ancient and resting head-down near the top of the stairs. Its iron head was caked in untold layers of rust but nonetheless bore a honed-enough edge to chop wood, albeit a bit imprecisely. Lifting it with my right hand, I found it weighed over ten pounds—it would be of no use to me for months, until my left arm healed enough to support a double-handed swing.

Setting the ax back beside the door, I walked down the steps and into the wild.

The cabin was set in a small clearing, the overgrown surroundings marked by rounded humps of granite-flecked quartz that broke the earth in scattered formations like a pod of whales. The silhouettes of treetops loomed over the clearing like apparitions in the mist, a ghostly presence watching me from all angles.

I chose to venture up the steepest hill to begin my exploration.

The specter of rolling white clouds parted at times to reveal vibrant green hills guarded by the spikes of a thousand pines slicing upward. At one point during my climb, the ground suddenly dropped away from me into a steep downward slope that extended a seeming eternity into a lush green valley, the mature pines dotting its depths appearing small as toothpicks. A wave of fog rolled in from one end of the valley, blanketing the forest below and giving me the feeling of sudden flight, as if I were looking down upon cloud formations.

My progress slowed as I neared the top of the hill beyond the cabin, where boulders rose into craggy formations, restricting my progress to damp, lichen-covered channels between them. Eventually I emerged above the mist and found a lake to sit beside, which would become a daily ritual for me during my time in isolation.

The placid crystal lake pooled in a neat circle that reflected the trees rising over it. At the far side, a break in the forest revealed a glimpse of distant mountain peaks, sun-bleached expanses of snow coating their slopes. Their beauty was mesmerizing, erasing from my mind the slings of my current plight and banishing the solitude, or at least allowing me to willingly embrace it for a time.

As I caught my breath from the uphill hike, a dark, looming cloud rolled overhead, creating a ceiling so low I could almost touch it. Something caught my eye, and I scanned the dark emerald formation of pine boughs and bushes until I made out the furry silhouette of a large gray canine head, wide-set eyes watching me closely.

The wolf whirled and vanished soundlessly into the forest, leaving a single swaying pine bough in its wake.

* * *

The fog didn't clear until nightfall. Innumerable stars twinkled beyond the blotted tree cover, pinpoints of light across a purple sky so startling that I remained outside long after my hands had lost feeling and my ears tingled with cold. I'd soon be able to venture inside, where winter clothing and a thermal sleeping bag would allow me to reclaim warmth. But for the moment, the sight above transfixed me after my long weeks of containment in the Mist Palace, after my path to execution had instead ended in the wilderness.

A guttural, otherworldly growling noise came from the forest behind me, turning my blood to ice. I ran to the cabin, snatching the ax beside the door and catching a glimpse of shifting darkness as I slammed the door shut.

My flesh was rippling with goose bumps, every hair standing on end as I heard something massive moving outside. The rustling of thicket was underscored by a low grunting, and I glanced out one of the ramshackle windows to see an immense black shape passing through the shadows. It must have been an adult grizzly, the curve of its back rising almost as tall as the cabin ceiling.

I clutched the ax with my right hand, feeling ridiculously impotent with my left arm contained by the sling—the ax was far too heavy to effectively swing one-handed under normal circumstances. But I reasoned that the surge of adrenaline following a grizzly breaking down the door would allow me at least one good blow before I was mauled to death and eaten.

I remained stock-still with my back to the flimsy cabin wall, facing the door with a white-knuckle grip on the ax handle for a seeming eternity until the bear completed its investigation and left. As the night fell silent, I waited for the hammering of my heart to subside and, finding that it didn't, remained awake with the ax in hand until the bleak golden glow of dawn seeped through the windows.

* * *

In my first week of solitude, I was periodically bumped by depression like driftwood floating at sea—that claustrophobia of the soul that revisited me, rendering the threshold of sleep an impenetrable wall, condemning me into isolation with my thoughts. No reprieve with alcohol, that magic elixir that made my waking hours interesting, fulfilling, bearable in so many ways that sobriety could not. I didn't suffer from depression—we simply coexisted. Together we were the last two patrons of a bar at closing time who decided to go to bed together for lack of options. Every night was a struggle of the mind, a flip of the coin to see if sleep would come or not, the mental pressure of walls closing in around me.

The songs of my incarceration were the rustling whistle of a mountain breeze through the cabin's edges backed by birdcalls by day and wolves howling by night. I yearned for bourbon, lusted for the golden-brown bottle the way a dying man sees a mirage in the desert. I remembered staggering through the sunset Somalian desert alongside Jais, being continually convinced that some forgotten store of water was contained in my meager belongings. Then I began fantasizing about suicide again. According to Sage, I could simply wander off into the woods and be torn apart by wild animals, and, barring that, the craggy outcroppings of the nearby cliff were more than sufficient—one last stand at the edge, a final BASE jump without a parachute.

By the second week I became intensely frustrated: with Sage, with my situation, with Ian's helplessness. With the Handler, though that much was nothing new. I began reliving moments of penetrating shame and doubt: betraying Parvaneh's trust, letting Ian get captured. Before Somalia he warned me I was too overconfident and underestimated the Handler's capabilities; before Brazil, it was my turn to warn Ian that he was being too brazen. Now we were both ensnared.

My mind became paranoid with delusions so repetitive that I had to remind myself aloud of what I knew to be true—otherwise, I'd find myself growing certain that Ian was already dead, that Sage had stuffed me into this cabin as part of some intricate plan concocted by the Handler, and, finally, that Sage wasn't returning at all. She'd been compromised and killed, or reassigned elsewhere, or had decided the suspicion against her was too great. In the event of any of those things occurring, I was going to survive here until the seasons warmed, then outfit myself for a cross-country hike toward the coast in a desperate bid to find civilization.

During my third week in the cabin, something broke in me. I'd wept in front of the little girl in the slums of Rio, an inexplicable reaction to nearly dying alongside her when a kill team had slipped past our hiding spot. For years before that, however, I simply couldn't remember crying. Yet during my isolation in the cabin, I cried not infrequently, though I had no idea why. Sometimes a grief-laced memory would evoke tears, and sometimes my eyes would sting at the sight of a particular wilderness vista. Or I'd be trying to go to sleep, thinking of nothing in particular, and feel my eyelashes growing wet.

At first I marked my time like a prisoner with a death sentence, countless miles of wilderness containing me as surely as cell bars. But by the fourth week, the delirious mental pressure of isolation began to lift. One day I simply awoke and flittered about the cabin and surrounding landscape with a lightness I'd never before known—devoid of anyone or anything requiring action, reaction, or appropriate conduct, I simply existed. It was as if the combination of wilderness, solitude, and sobriety had caused my mind to process and reconcile much of the pain endemic to my existence.

The stack of paperbacks Sage had left for me became a welcome reprieve, a distant touch point, however fictional, to people, to civilization, to the web of human relationships that I was stranded from. And so before each sunset, I would re-enter my cabin to read by headlamp until sleep came at last.

5

Six Weeks in Isolation
March 16, 2009

It took Sage longer than a month to return. Forty-four days, by my count, and I had few commitments beyond physical therapy and adding hash marks to a mildewed piece of wood on the cabin's interior wall.

I was lucky to hear the faint approach of her ATV—it was shortly before noon, and I was clambering down the slope from my now-daily visit to the hilltop lake.

I walked around the front of the cabin just as she pulled up, the flat black ATV hauling at a fast clip before she braked and entered a sideways skid that brought her to a sliding halt after ten feet.

The sight of her was dizzying, the very glimpse of a fellow human sending me into an almost delirious sense of full-body bliss. I became acutely concerned about my ability to communicate well, whether my voice would be raspy from disuse. My words felt awkward and clunky as I called, "Welcome back to Casa de Rivers. You really know how to handle that vehicle."

She dismounted her ATV, a fleece jacket hugging her curves. She sported a long ponytail, frail threads of hair displaced from her ride.

She brushed a loose tendril of red hair behind an ear. "One of many such skills."

"Don't tease me."

"I never tease, David. And you're supposed to be in your sling for another week."

I flexed the fingers on my newly liberated left hand. "Must've misread the instructions."

"*C'est la vie.* I like the beard—it's a good look for you. Help me unload some supplies, I don't have much time."

I strode down to the ATV, then assisted her in unstrapping the boxes attached to the rear. I caught a whiff of her shampoo, and the scent was tantalizing in its novelty. My sense of smell had become uncannily acute while at the cabin. I unequivocally knew, sight unseen, when a badger or wolverine was near—the faintest trace of musky odor was as detectable to me as a blast from a foghorn.

To my embarrassment, the boxes were too heavy for me to support their weight with my still-healing left arm. Instead I grabbed a single box with my right and, following Sage into the cabin, asked, "How is Ian?"

"He's well."

"I want proof that he's alive."

She set her boxes down and turned to me with an incredulous smile. "Proof? You misunderstand your situation, David. And mine. I'm your only link to the world outside of this wilderness, and I placed myself in grave danger to save your life."

I leaned against the cabin wall, folding my arms. "I didn't ask for your charity."

"This isn't charity, it's a business transaction. I invested in your survival because when the time comes, I'll need you to perform a very specific task for me. Ian's life is leverage to achieve that, and while I will make good on freeing him if—and only if—you perform your mission as ordered, that doesn't put you in any position to make demands."

"I'll perform whatever the hell you want, *if* Ian is alive. What's to say he's not dead already?"

Sage examined my eyes, seemingly taken aback at my suspicion. "The Handler doesn't waste talent, David. Ian is very much alive and working in the Intelligence Directorate. Your concern should be whether he'll want to be freed. After a time, people begin working for the Handler of their own volition—they go from slaves to willing servants."

"Ian will never turn. He hates the Handler more than anyone."

"There's an analyst who's been there for five years who started as a captured spy. He's quite happy now."

I shook my head distantly. By the Handler's own admission, Ian had successfully evaded surveillance for months, right up until the moment of his capture. If anyone was smart enough to defy the Handler from within, it was Ian.

"All right," I conceded. "So Ian is alive and gainfully employed. What about Parvaneh?"

Now it was Sage's turn to cross her arms, squaring off against me with a piercing glare. "Are you in love with the princess?"

"Hilarious. How is she?"

"Miserable. The Handler was never so distraught as when she was missing in Rio. He hasn't let her or her daughter, Langley, leave the Mist Palace since."

"Does Parvaneh think I'm dead?"

Sage balked at the question. "Rest assured, she has not forgotten about you, and I don't mean that she thinks of you fondly. She was waiting for me to draft my statement about your death, then snatched it from me before I could deliver it to the Intelligence Directorate. I think her only disappointment was that she couldn't kill you herself."

The words caused a spike of shame within me. It was inevitable, I supposed—by using her favor to attempt to assassinate her father, I'd deceived her beyond the point of recognition.

"Moving swiftly on," I changed the subject, "your supply run seems a little light."

"There's new books, and—"

"I'm not concerned about reading material."

"I brought you some fresh food, figured you'd be tired of the field rations—"

"There's something I want from you, Sage, and it's not food."

An eyebrow shot up as her demeanor shifted from professional to amused. "That's very forward of you, David. Have you spent too much time in the woods?"

"I wouldn't kick you out of bed for eating crackers, Sage. But that's not what I'm talking about. I keep listening for liquid sloshing in one of these boxes."

"I didn't bring you any vodka."

"Good, because I'm hoping for bourbon. And thank you for saving me, but abandoning me in the cold clutches of sobriety seems a cruel fate."

She shrugged indifferently. "You appear to be making do."

"Well," I muttered, "if there's no booze and your clothes are staying on, let's move to priority number three. Shall we start planning the Handler's death?"

"Planning?" She released a muffled gasp of laughter as she lifted herself to sit atop a stack of boxed rations.

"Something funny?"

"You're a shooter, not a strategist."

"There's more to being a shooter than killing people. I'd challenge you to react to a five-man hit team like I did in Rio."

Her brow wrinkled in an expression of skepticism, but she said nothing.

"All right," I admitted, "so humility has never been my strong suit. But still."

"So you're a strategist, are you? Then tell me, how would you kill the Handler?"

I palmed my beard around my chin, delivering the response I'd contemplated many times in the past six weeks of isolation. "Poison."

"The Handler has state-of-the-art medical supplies and a doctor on standby capable of treating the most severe and fatal of injuries, as a further prevention against assassination." She managed a tight smile, continuing, "Therefore, your poison must not only be exotic enough to bypass the Handler's cutting-edge security screening but also potent enough to cause irreversible death. You have any substance like that on hand?"

"No, but if you created a replica truck and faked my death with a body double, then you've got the means."

"Assuming we came into possession of such a substance, how would you administer it?" She watched me closely, though I couldn't tell if she was trying to determine whether I was a plaything, an adversary, or both.

"At the Executive *Karoga*. On the night I went, there would have been plenty of time to place something in the pot."

"Wrong. The food is safeguarded on its way to and from the dining site, the bodyguards are present at all times, and the meal is shared, so you've just killed the entire executive staff needed to run operations. Next?"

"Then we hit him while he's alone in his office. Remotely."

"Brilliant. How?"

"Explosives."

She cringed, giving a sad shake of her head. "The security screenings will detect the faintest trace of explosive long before it reaches the perimeter wall, much less his building. And since the Organization is involved in every facility that manufactures substances for high-level assassinations, trust that his security is on the very cutting edge of what's available. But," she added in an upbeat tone, "you're on the right track with doing it remotely. Did you notice the red pipes on his office ceiling?"

I thought back to my view from the chair facing his desk, where I had observed the crimson cylinder snaking from corner to corner above.

"Yes." I nodded. "A water or foam system? To extinguish fires in case anyone tries to kill him that way?"

"The pipes aren't there to extinguish a fire; they're there to ensure it."

"I don't understand."

"Instead of building a vault for his sensitive information, he built a vault around his office." Her pitch was one of admiration, underscoring a begrudging reverence of this unconventional security measure. "Should the Mist Palace ever be attacked, the office serves as his safe room. And if the fort is overrun, the Handler can incinerate his office—and himself—with the touch of an eight-digit code."

"Then we can hack it. Burn him alive while he's inside."

"The code is known only to him and his personal bodyguard."

"So we turn Racegun into an ally."

She seemed aggravated by my suggestion. "He has absolute allegiance to the office. It's why he was chosen."

"There has to be a way to turn him. Especially for a woman of your...abilities."

"Don't get cute. You don't understand the loyalty this organization breeds. It is beyond a cult."

"I got that impression by their use of the word 'vicar.'" I drummed my fingers against one leg, trying to think. "What about hitting the Handler while he's outside his building?"

"The grounds are monitored by motion sensors and thermal cameras. There's also a curfew at the Mist Palace, and the Handler only travels outside when it's in effect. And when he moves, his personal security detail is augmented by an exterior transport team armed with assault rifles."

"Then where is he both unaccompanied and outside his office?"

"There is only one place the Handler or Parvaneh ventures alone, free from the immediate presence of guards."

"Where?"

Sage shook her head, responding firmly, "You're the self-proclaimed strategist, David. You tell me."

I glanced about the cabin, mind flipping through what little I'd seen of the Mist Palace as I searched for the answer.

"The garden," I said abruptly. "The fortress within a fortress that I saw after coming back from Rio—isolated by a wall, with barbed wire on top and guards at the entrance."

"Precisely." She seemed surprised that I guessed correctly. "But the garden perimeter is too heavily guarded. You're looking for a simpler solution to assassinate him."

"Let's see," I began, thoughtfully tapping my beard with an index finger, "vast bodyguard force with unquestionable loyalty, a curfew, advanced chemical sensors that can detect poison and explosives... Whatever the answer is, I wouldn't describe it as 'simple.'"

Sage shrugged unapologetically. "Simple doesn't mean cheap, nor easy to acquire."

"So it's expensive and difficult to acquire—what's your plan to overcome that?"

"I can manage the expense. The difficulty to acquire...well, David, that's where you come in."

"You need a shooter."

"I might," she admitted, clenching her jaw as if troubled by this potential requirement. "More immediately, I need someone with your psychological profile, screened for the ability to conduct violence and maintain secrets, which the Outfit has well established from your selection process. Further, you have the motivation to kill the Handler at all costs—which, by definition, means the Handler is aware of you and therefore safeguarded against your best efforts. As you found out after Rio."

"Unless the Handler thinks I'm dead."

"Which is why I went to great risk to feign your execution."

I drew a breath and supplied, "And now you need me to recover something."

"When it's ready."

"What is it?"

"An element integral to the assassination attempt. It's not ready yet, but when it is, I'll need you prepared to do everything I say."

My voice swelled with assurance. "If it will free Ian, there's nothing that will stop me."

"Good," she said, checking her watch, "because I have to go. My absence can't be noted for too long. I'll never be fully beyond suspicion."

"Until the Handler's dead."

"Until the Handler's dead," she agreed.

"Who will take the throne when he's gone, and what do you get out of this?"

She ignored my question. "I'll be back as soon as the item is ready for you to recover. If that takes longer than a month, I'll come by to bring you some provisions and check on your sanity."

I briefly wondered how much of what she had told me was true, then said, "Come back to me soon, Sage. It gets lonely out here."

Her body stiffened at this comment, but she said nothing as she slipped out the door, casting me a final rearward glance that found my eyes locked on her in quiet desperation.

6

Three Months in Isolation
May 12, 2009

By the arrival of my birthday I was a professional camper.

In contrast to my early weeks at the cabin, the white-noise hum of my depression had subsided while in the wilderness. I now knew my surroundings from long hikes that ranged farther and farther from the cabin, gradually extending so far that I pushed the bounds of my ability to return by nightfall. These trips yielded no traces of human presence beyond the ATV trail continuing much farther than I could cover on foot. Instead I was met with only elk sightings, bear scat, or bald eagles and the occasional osprey watching me from treetop perches or while soaring between blanketed patches of mist. Once I crossed cougar tracks by a streambed, the muddy impressions betraying the passage of a mother and two cubs.

Now, my twenty-sixth birthday was commemorated with a dinner little different than any other I'd had in the mountains: a ration supplemented with a two-pound trout I'd caught while stream fishing that afternoon.

I was preparing my food, the sun setting over the Cascades, when I heard the faint noise of Sage's ATV. By the time I'd left the cabin she was already stopping her vehicle outside, and I approached to unstrap the supply boxes as she killed the engine.

I watched the movement of her body as she dismounted the vehicle. After a month in the wilderness, any woman with a slightly feminine physique would have looked incredible. But after crossing my hundredth day in isolation—an event that transpired the previous morning—a road cone would have looked pretty good.

"Is it time?" I asked, sliding my gaze up the curves of her figure to meet her stare.

"Our item isn't ready yet—we must continue to be patient, David." She stopped abruptly, her liquid gray eyes scanning mine. "You're looking much healthier. Vibrant, even."

She was right, I knew. After a few weeks out of my sling, I was taking tentative jogs on flat ground. After a month, I was able to execute uphill scrambles to my mountaintop lake. By now, I could even swing the heavy ax to chop firewood with relative ease.

"Bonding with nature, I suppose." I hefted a stack of boxes and transferred them into the cabin. Once inside, she unslung her backpack and handed me two photographs from within.

"Do you recognize these two, David?"

I scanned the faces in the photos. One was a nerdy-looking man, the other a woman with long frumpy hair who could have passed for a librarian.

"How could I forget? They were waiting when I returned from Somalia."

"Did you learn what was in the case that the Handler sent you there to get?"

"A billet of highly enriched uranium. Jais said it was sold in Ukraine but went missing as it crossed the Black Sea. It came up for sale in the black market of Yemen just before our mission."

"All correct. And these two"—she took the photographs back from me, replacing them in her bag—"are nuclear engineers. They were present to take control of the case and verify its contents."

"So?"

Setting her backpack on the floor, she hoisted herself atop the stack of boxed rations, stretching her long legs from the ATV ride. "They were flown to the Mist Palace last week."

"Jais said the Handler was buying the uranium to get it off the black market. You're telling me he's turned it into a weapon?"

"He's turned it into a potentially valuable resource for the war in South America, but he's refusing to employ it. And the Organization loses legitimacy with each day that passes without defeating the opposition, particularly when any possible configuration of players could be uniting to defeat us."

Weighing her words in my mind, I took a seat on the boxes opposite her. "Killing the Handler will help the opposition to succeed, not suppress them."

"Wrong," she corrected. "The Handler is growing soft. Listening to prophecies, failing to retaliate properly when his daughter was almost killed in Brazil. The person taking power will be more suited to deal with insurrection than the Handler is. The new leader will restore order, starting with a global message that will assure the Organization's legitimacy for another century."

I found myself shaking my head in disbelief. "Who is more brutal than the Handler?"

She smiled, neatly crossing her arms under her breasts. "That's not your concern at present."

"So what happens to Parvaneh when your assassination plot occurs?"

"Don't get sentimental. She lacks the resolution to carry out the position she seeks to inherit."

"You didn't answer my question," I persisted.

Sage nearly rolled her eyes at me. "As much as I would love to eliminate that snowflake altogether, we can't do so without being overrun with retaliatory assassination attempts. We'll employ Parvaneh in the modernization efforts befitting the legitimacy she so desperately seeks to create, and she in turn has no choice but to maintain the reputation of the Organization." She breathed a sharp sigh of resignation. "And I must admit, she has the makings of a fine negotiator. You can never have too many of those on your side in this business."

"If you succeed," I began, examining the calluses on my right palm, "I want my role in her father's death to be kept secret from her. I've hurt Parvaneh enough. Just free Ian, send me to the Complex, and keep me in combat." I met Sage's gray eyes, framed by long lashes that required no makeup to accentuate her beauty. "Deal?"

"Deal," she agreed without hesitation. Then she lowered her voice and continued, "But take the 'if' out of this plot—I don't want to hear you express doubt ever again."

"Let's face it: even if you succeed in assassinating the Handler, you're probably going to be killed. There are too many bodyguards for anyone to get close enough and then survive."

"Bodyguards protect the Handler's seat, not the individual. If an assassin bypasses their efforts, they'll protect the victor."

I almost laughed at this revelation. "You've got to be kidding."

"To the contrary—since the Organization's inception, power has changed hands many times in exactly this way. Including by the current Handler."

"But what if someone unqualified succeeds?" I countered. "The Organization would collapse."

Sage's critical glance indicated I'd missed some vital element that explained this seeming contradiction. "No, David. Order would soon be restored by another assassination conspiracy."

I leaned forward on my box, nodding slowly. "So that's the reasoning behind the insane level of security at the Mist Palace..."

"Yes."

"...the handcuffs, blacked-out goggles, bodyguards stationed all over the compound...they're not worried about an outside attack. They're worried about an inside one."

"Exactly." She flashed me a wide smile, her approval eliciting a warm rush of emotion within me. "Welcome to the arena, David. Why did you think the Handler is never referred to by a birth name? Or seen by anyone outside the highest levels of power?"

I shrugged. "I assumed it was because he's a giant asshole."

"It's to maintain international legitimacy. The Organization has eclipsed every barrier of language and culture to unify a global network of criminal groups. That alone requires a single organization at the top that observes no borders, no criminal fealty other than its own." Then she shook her head solemnly and concluded, "No kingpin or cartel leader is above the Handler, whoever that may be at the time."

"But that criminal network dissolves into chaos if the Handler's position is known to be compromised."

"Not just the criminal network, David, but the *legal* one."

I scrutinized her face for a possible explanation. "What's legal about any of this?"

"Only the Organization's investors—legitimate executives and politicians. The Organization offers a fully laundered return on their investment at rates that, like the cocaine trade, transcend all economies of scale."

"I wasn't under the impression that major crime moguls were hurting on cash in the first place."

"The Handler doesn't need their cash," Sage answered pointedly, "he needs their *knowledge*. Investors are chosen for their ability to inform us on government initiatives that will affect criminal endeavors—infrastructure, railways, maritime routes, trade agreements, even legislation that will take years to impact illegal operations."

"So that's how the Organization stays ahead of the game, how they've never been dismantled..."

"By incentivizing industry conversion to things like synthetic drugs, appeasing policymakers, and negotiating between politicians and criminal groups worldwide. Whoever occupies the Handler's throne pulls the strings to order which loads of narcotics will be interdicted, what kingpin will be arrested, and which corrupt politicians will be exposed, all while keeping the real players on both sides of the legality fence safe."

My thoughts swept back to the Handler's daughter, unable to reconcile her perceived role in the dark underworld she stood to inherit. "I don't understand how Parvaneh believed she could ever legitimize any of that. On our way back from Brazil, she told me that once she took over, she'd use her power to help people."

"The Organization exploits the fracture lines of weak governance— oppressive regimes, corrupt intelligence agencies, under-administered regions. In poverty-stricken areas, the network can provide economic prosperity—legitimate jobs in shadow corporations, manufacturing facilities run legitimately to provide money laundering and a front for the movement of illicit products. You understand now?"

"No, I don't. Because if that's true, why couldn't Parvaneh succeed in legitimizing the Organization, at least partially?"

Sage seemed frustrated at my inability to grasp her point. "Because the ensuing loss of profit would upset the wrong people. She'd be assassinated, and order restored. And this fairy tale inside her mind is one of many reasons that she is an unsuitable successor."

"So why do you want the Handler dead—is it just about power?"

"Why do *you* want him dead, David?"

"For enslaving Ian."

She tilted her head, her tone unrepentant. "That's the consequence of Ian's assassination attempt. Ian went head-to-head, and he lost. Fair play. Why else do you hate the Handler?"

"He killed my entire mercenary team," I pointed out. "And Karma."

"Which was an elegant solution."

I shot off the box, rising to my full standing height over her. "What does that mean?"

"Langley is the Handler's granddaughter. Langley's father was Roshan."

My pulse quickened as I shot back, "Boss's team thought that—"

"It doesn't matter what they thought," she began, completely unfazed by my sudden change in disposition, "it matters what they did. And they killed Roshan. The Handler didn't find that out until your team was close to eliminating his domestic opposition element, the Five Heads. The Handler was, as always, facing a wide bevy of internal and external threats to his reign."

I fought the urge to begin pacing the cabin, instead glowering at Sage as she continued, "To avenge Roshan's death too late would be an outrage to many. To do so too early would leave the Five Heads to continue gaining market share in open defiance. The Handler's solution allowed your team to eliminate the opposition, punished their transgression at the completion of their final job, and kept his daughter from learning the horrible truth about her lover's death. What would *you* have done in his place, David?"

I didn't answer her, instead looking away with a mounting sense of rage.

My thoughts were darkened by her flippant references to Karma and my dead teammates, the cold logic with which she appraised Ian's captivity.

She stood and placed a soothing hand on my bicep, her voice suddenly compassionate. "I don't mean to get you worked up about the past. I've got some time before I have to go if you want to...unwind."

I jerked my arm away, stepping back from her. "I think we should keep it professional until the job is done."

"Impressive restraint considering you've been alone in the woods for months on end."

"Just a matter of priorities," I said tersely. "Don't take offense."

She seemed to have expected my response, her tone undaunted as if she relished the challenge to her proposal. "I don't. Seduction is like assassination—every target has a vulnerability."

"Let me know when you find mine."

"Believe me, David," she said with a charming smile, "I already have."

"Bourbon doesn't count."

Sage's smile faded into a wintry glare. "I'm not talking about bourbon. There's another vulnerability with you, and it reaches far deeper into your psyche than alcohol."

She turned and walked out before I could respond, and despite the anger that still hammered in my veins, I watched her depart with a mournful sense of dread at being abandoned once again.

7

Six Months in Isolation
August 20, 2009

I'd retired to the cabin as the landscape began assuming the eerie auburn hue of sunset, not wanting to take my chances with the wolves and grizzlies that roamed freely amid the darkness. As I was preparing my headlamp and a well-worn paperback Western for a nighttime reading session, I heard the thin buzz of an all-terrain vehicle approaching.

I stood in the doorway as Sage's ATV appeared and came to a stop. She killed the engine as I called to her, "Is the item ready?"

"Almost," she answered. "It's in transit."

"To where?"

"You don't need to know."

"Yesterday was my two hundredth day here," I said, walking over to help her with the resupply. "I'm running out of space in the cabin to carve hash marks. You can at least tell me where I'll be headed when the item arrives."

She gracefully swung a leg over the ATV to dismount, rising to her full height and flexing her back after the long drive. Her crimson hair assumed an almost fire-like luminosity in the waning sun, her long ponytail flipped sideways as she turned to unstrap a resupply box.

"All right, David. You'll be headed to Myanmar."

I took the box from her, our eyes meeting for a fleeting moment. "You mean Burma?"

"Formerly." She led the way into the cabin, and I set my box atop a stack of field rations and waited for an explanation.

When one didn't come, I asked, "Why Myanmar, of all places?"

"Of all places? Where did you think your destination would be, David, the French Riviera? A casino in Montenegro?"

"Well, if it's on the table—"

"Myanmar is a case study in national crime. Their largest business conglomerate was *founded* as a front for heroin trafficking. By the time Western nations were imposing sanctions, the conglomerate's reach extended across Southeast Asia via a half dozen otherwise legitimate enterprises growing with billions from foreign investment."

"So...what? An organization in Myanmar is the Handler's new competition?"

"Competition?"

"Why else would the item you need to assassinate him be coming from there?"

"How thick can you be?" She cursed under her breath and muttered, "What kind of man did I rescue?"

My shoulders straightened defensively. "You've got a lot of balls insulting me," I began, hearing the raw nerves in my voice, "when I've been sitting up here blindly trusting in this brilliant plan of yours—"

"Myanmar isn't competition; the Handler is going to mint his own money there. Now that China is building oil and gas pipelines through Myanmar, the Organization is acquiring rights to explore for natural resources through shadow companies based in a half-dozen underdeveloped countries in three continents. If the estimates on oil and gas reserves are remotely accurate, the Organization stands to earn 1.2 billion dollars in the next decade. That's billion with a B, from one compartmentalized project. I wouldn't be surprised if there were hundreds more that I'm not privy to. *That's* the kind of power the Organization deals in, David. Start getting that through your head, if you're capable."

I felt my hands flex into fists. "Listen, Sage—"

She cut me off, stepping closer. "What, are you going to hit me now?"

"Believe me, sweetheart, if I hit you, you wouldn't know whether to—"

Her first punch caught me on the left cheekbone, sending my head snapping back.

She then delivered a sharp uppercut to my stomach, knocking the wind out of me and doubling me over. I launched forward in a rage, spearing her into the ground and straddling her to deliver a downward blow toward her face.

She diverted my fist to the side, trapping my arm and planting one foot while using the opposite leg to effortlessly roll me over. As my back slammed into the ground, I locked my thighs around her waist, momentarily distracted by a glimpse of creamy white cleavage. She rapidly boxed my ear, and the crushing cartilage pain flung me back to my present struggle.

I threw a punch at her face—she dodged, but too late, and my fist glanced off the side of her head. As she recoiled from the partial blow, she swung a jab toward my nose. I blocked it with both forearms, and then cracked my elbow into her stomach.

She collapsed on top of me, breasts smothering my face, and slid her arms around my neck. I took a sharp breath and held it as she delivered a crushing squeeze against my larynx—the smart thing to do would have been to break her choke. Instead, I grabbed a fistful of her ponytail and jerked her head backward so hard that she yelped in pain. Using my opposite hand, I slapped her across the face as hard as anyone had ever slapped another human being, and she rolled off to the side.

I scrambled to my feet, intending on rearranging her facial structure with my boot, but by the time I was half-upright she was already in a fighting stance, bouncing lightly on the balls of her feet before delivering a roundhouse kick to my head.

Flying backwards, I crashed into the stack of field rations. Grabbing the plastic ties of the top cardboard box, I heaved it sideways in a wide, curving arc and flung it toward Sage.

She easily sidestepped the flying box, which crashed into the shaky wood wall as we charged into each other. I went low, tackling her around the waist and flinging us both to the ground. She landed on all fours, and I used the opportunity to slap her ass.

Scrambling away, she kicked me hard in the shoulder. I grabbed her leg before she could withdraw it, and for reasons unknown to me even to this day, I bit her calf like a determined terrier.

"Bastard!" she cried in a girlish yell, twisting away and kicking me in the eyebrow with her other leg.

I scrambled backward and yelled back, "Fuckin' harlot!"

She was atop me in a flash, mounting my chest with her knees in my armpits, restricting my ability to punch. Her hands were around my throat, choking me forcefully—but her face was flushed, lips parted, eyes ablaze with an almost irrational desire.

Releasing her wrists, I grabbed her flannel shirtfront and ripped it open, buttons scattering to the floor. She thrust her face into mine and kissed me. Her hands released my neck and I grabbed hers, rolling her over as she fumbled with my belt.

We stripped our clothes off and tumbled into lovemaking like falling down a mountain, the momentum of our fight seamlessly transitioning into an equal fury of lust. She was passionate and experienced, matching my enthusiasm as we crashed around the darkening cabin.

We fell into a synchronized rhythm, adapting to each other's bodies as if we'd been lovers for months instead of minutes. Her eyes were fixed on mine until the sun set completely, when I was left with only the feel of her body, the hotness of her breath on my neck, her velvet lips panting against my mouth. Her thumb grazed the tender skin over my left cheekbone, and seeing me flinch, she applied more pressure—pain interlaced with ecstasy.

"Sage," I whispered breathlessly, all other words escaping me as her lips met mine. I tensed and shuddered, every ounce of energy expended as I collapsed at the finish. My entire body felt tingling and numb as she kissed me softly, caressing the side of my head, running her fingers down my face.

We fell into a deep sleep in each other's arms, our limbs intertwined within my sleeping bag.

* * *

I burst awake with a sense of imminent disaster. A hand clamped against my mouth, forcing my head to the ground as I felt the curved, paper-thin edge of a blade pressed beneath my jaw.

Sage was fully clothed, her powerful thighs straddling me as she hunched over my face like a jungle cat landing from a pounce. I could barely make out her features in the darkness but felt her hot breath upon my face as she whispered, "Seduction is like assassination—every target has a vulnerability. And yours, David Rivers, is *violence*." The pulse in my jugular throbbed against the pressure from the blade, which was tight enough to break skin at any second. "I can do this to every politician, mob boss, and business titan in the world. You want to know who is more brutal than the Handler—who is going to assume the throne?"

Her voice lowered to a rasping howl. "*I am.*"

She raised the knife and brought it back down in a swift overhand stabbing motion, spearing the blade into the wooden plank beside my head.

Her weight was off me in a flash, and I caught a glimpse of her shadow slipping out the doorway.

I sat up, gasping, as the ATV fired up and raced away down the trail. Taking a few panting breaths, I looked from the open door to the knife impaled beside me, then pressed two fingers to my jugular and pulled them away to feel a fine line of hot blood.

With a final breath, I collapsed back down to the floor and gasped three words to the ceiling:

"What. The. *Hell*."

* * *

After sunrise I took the rusty ax and went behind the cabin to use it.

It wasn't that I needed more firewood—instead, each heaving chop of the ax, each pop of the log sections into neatly split wedges, each *thunk* of my ax blade into the surface of the stump forced my mind into the present moment. I swung the ax with an easy violence that represented an outlet I so desperately craved.

There would be no placidly staring off into the hilltop lake this morning, no wistfully glimpsing the snow-covered mountains in the distance.

JASON KASPER

My thoughts were a mob of frantic people crushing one another in a bid to escape. Almost seven months in isolation spent passing from depression to near inner peace, and now I felt on the brink of a nervous breakdown.

I brought the ax downward, splitting the log apart and wedging my blade firmly into the stump. Wrenching the ax head free, I reached for another log and chopped it in two.

As the wood exploded, I heard the ATV approaching once more. Great, I thought—what would she want now? We have sex and she virtually threatens to kill me, ending her monologue with the fact that she's going to be the next Handler, as if I gave a shit—once Ian was free, my only concern was rejoining the Outfit and shipping off to war in South America. And now, here she was, back the next day as if none of that had happened.

The ATV stopped opposite the cabin, and I raised the ax over my head one more time. My vision was fixed on the concentric circles of the weathered stump before me, its flat surface scarred with a hundred ax strikes. I swung a mighty blow downward to elicit the hollow *thunk* of the blade wedging firmly into the wood.

Then, leaving it there, I strode angrily around the cabin, equal parts eager for and dreading the confrontation with Sage. Before I rounded the corner I heard her calling my name, sounding anxious and almost fearful —what an act. She'd already stashed me in the cabin and played her mind games to prove I'd sleep with her. Was this her next manipulation?

I rounded the corner to see her still seated on the ATV and looking around frantically. Her eyes found mine and she nearly shouted at me, "Get on! The item has almost reached Myanmar. You have to fly today."

8

Three Days Later
August 24, 2009
Lashio, Myanmar

"Wait here. He will arrive soon."

My contact closed the door, encapsulating me in a solitary room whose windows had been covered with newspaper from the inside. The temporary safe house was an ostensibly derelict business, a central location easily accessible from the Lashio airport, where I'd just arrived on a cargo flight.

I strolled to the patchwork of newspaper sections, the sheets forming a mosaic of spindly, ornate Burmese and Chinese script. Finding a gap in the paper, I peered through the rain-streaked window, gaining my first real glimpse of Myanmar after being transported aboard a delivery truck to the safe house.

The view revealed storefronts, balconies, and walkways teeming with palm trees and bushes. Between the brightly colored signs and heavily planted infrastructure, the center of Lashio looked like an urban rainforest. Whereas the people in the Rio favela I'd visited seemed to be surviving in the most densely packed of slums, the population in Myanmar was thriving. Despite a steady downpour of rain, the streets bustled with peaceful activity, the people walking lightly beneath their umbrellas without a care in the world, their clothes as colorful as any Westerner on a tropical vacation. While nothing about my surroundings spoke to wealth or luxury, the town was bright and happy despite the rain, not a scrap of trash to be seen. Sure, I'd sweated through all my clothes already in the Southeast Asian humidity, but I appreciated the bizarrely resort-like ambiance.

My calm fascination at the sight surprised me.

Like many who have experienced combat, I harbored an inherent discomfort around large crowds. In war the civilian populace represents a sea of possible enemy informants and hidden fighters, any group of people outside your team intrinsically tied with decreased control and increased danger. Once that correlation becomes etched in the fabric of your psyche —a mere handful of ambushes or explosions will do the trick—you tend to carry that perception forward across the rest of your life.

Yet after spending so long in isolation in the remote wilderness of British Columbia, the sheer number and density of people in Lashio was more bewildering to me than fear-inducing. After all, I'd just spent half a year speaking to no human but Sage, and neither her nor I were normal in any sense of the word.

So why was I in Myanmar?

Sage wouldn't say. The item was about to arrive, but I didn't need to know what it was or why it was in this corner of the world. Get the item, David. Ian's freedom depends upon it, and so does yours. Don't give me that shit, Sage. I'll get your item, but you owe me some answers.

But she provided none.

I heard the door open behind me and turned, expecting to see the man who'd dropped me off.

Instead an Asian boy of perhaps fifteen years old entered, carrying a black canvas bag in one hand.

He made fleeting eye contact and then looked at the floor, beginning to speak and then falling silent as if he found me intimidating.

"How's it going, buddy?" I asked.

He nodded and sheepishly lowered his eyes.

"English?"

"Hello." He nodded again.

"You lost?"

He shook his head.

"Is my contact here yet?"

"I...I am your contact, Mr. David." He handed me the black satchel, and I took it by a canvas grip—it weighed close to twenty pounds.

"Is this my item?"

"It is her refund. In full. 640,000 US. My grandfather sends his deepest regrets."

I threw the bag down at his feet. "I didn't come here for a refund. I came here for my item."

"It happened while you were on the flight."

"What happened?"

He sheepishly rubbed a slender bicep. "The government invaded Laukkai."

"Laukkai?"

"In the Kokang region. Near China border."

"And?"

"They seized the facility with your item. Most of the population has fled to China. Laukkai is occupied by government troops. Shops are closed, internet cut off. Laukkai has become a town of ghosts."

"You mean ghost town."

"Even the Kokang leader has fled, and it is unclear if he will attack the Myanmarese."

"Aren't you all Myanmarese?"

"Kokang is Han Chinese. In fifty years, the junta cannot control the border region—we do. With our armies. The junta is trying to—"

"Junta?"

"Myanmar Army. They try and disarm our forces and turn us into a border guard."

"If you've been independent so long, why the sudden change?"

"Next year. The national election..."

"I get it," I interjected, cutting him off with a wave of my hand. "Same story every time a regime subjugates the rebellious part of its population. Not a lot of political legitimacy to be claimed when an entire region refuses to participate, right?"

He squinted at me, struggling to comprehend one or more of my words. I simplified, "Kokang has always ruled Kokang, and now the government wants to control you? Ethnic Burmese versus ethnic Chinese?"

"Yes." He nodded excitedly. "Yes. Now you understand. Your item is in junta possession, and they will burn it with everything else whenever they leave."

I closed my eyes and drew a long breath, formulating what I'd have to do in the time it took me to finish inhaling. But first I'd need to find the real decision maker, not the messenger.

I rolled my head to the side, cracking my neck. "What's your name, brother?"

"I am Cong."

"Cong, you need to let me speak with whoever is in charge."

"My cousin is waiting outside—"

"Not your cousin. I mean whoever is in charge of my employer's order for this item. That person."

"He is not here. It is forbidden for you to speak to him."

"We'll see about that. Go fetch your cousin, if he's the highest-ranking person here."

Cong bowed his head and backed out the door, closing it behind him and leaving the bag of money on the floor. Amateur, I thought. Maybe they all were—I'd just come to retrieve an order worth over a half-million dollars, and they'd sent a child to deliver Sage's refund and apology.

Cong opened the door and re-entered with the words, "This is my cousin, Tiao."

Then he stepped aside to make way for a thickly muscled Burmese man with a square jaw. He was nearly my height, making him taller than every Myanmarese I'd seen since arriving.

"Nice to meet you, Tiao."

Tiao's eyes ticked downward to the bag of money, then back up to me. He looked offended by my presence, and spat a long string of Chinese at a chagrined Cong.

I gestured to my ear. "Can you speak English, please? So I may understand."

Tiao folded thick forearms across his chest. "My cousin had one job.

This first time we trust him, talk to client. Once his grandfather hear of failure, the last."

"Tiao," I said, "this is not Cong's fault. He explained the situation. But the woman who sent me entrusted a great deal of money to obtain this item."

"My people made sacrifice—money just one. Great effort, lives lost. Gain and transport item. Only for junta seize it."

"My employer and I are deeply grateful for your efforts, and those of your people. Does the junta know that they have the item?"

He shook his head with grave import. "No. It is hidden. If your employer care, she answer phone."

I conceded, "She's rarely in a position to accept calls. So it will be more appropriate if I discuss the situation with the highest decision maker before I depart."

Tiao unfolded his arms to thrust an index finger into my sternum, rocking me back on my heels as he spoke. "If boss want speak to you, America, he be here. Not me."

I shook my head in response, though I'd have to tread lightly. I was a stranger in a strange land, and this guy was simultaneously in control and pissed off—I could handle one or the other, but both at once was a tricky proposition. "There must be many dangers in traveling cross-country for a man of his status. I do not ask for him to come here. Instead, please take me to him. Allow me one conversation, and then I will take the refund and leave."

"You have no right," he countered, frowning at my persistence.

"That is his decision to make. If I bring my employer a refund without speaking to your boss in person, she will demand a meeting with him."

"*If* he want speak, then you drive. Five hour to him. To meet, maybe five minute. Then five hour back. No better off."

"I would then depart," I pointed out, "able to inform my employer that I was met with the greatest courtesy and personally briefed by the man who accepted the commission for the item. This will satisfy her acceptance of the refund, and our business will be complete."

Tiao's massive jaw settled firmly as he watched me with contempt.

Then he produced a cell phone and dialed, holding it to his ear. Cong had been shamed to silence, studying the floor as Tiao's call connected and he conversed in Chinese. The entire call lasted less than a minute, after which he hung up and pocketed the phone, looking to me.

"You get wish. We now drive ten hour. For my boss to tell you same thing, in different voice." His lips curved into a sarcastic grin. "Fine job, America."

* * *

We exited into a back alley, walking through warm rain and slipping into a tiny parked sedan. Tiao struggled to lower himself into the passenger seat with the bag of cash while I did the same in the back, my shoulder almost touching Cong beside me in the cramped vehicle. A bad pothole would cause my head to bang on the ceiling.

A driver was behind the wheel, older than Cong but younger than Tiao. Maybe mid-twenties, I guessed. He looked back with a cheerful expression that turned to stone when he saw me getting into the backseat. He glared at Tiao, who said something in Chinese before nodding toward Cong. Cong, looking humiliated and ashamed, gazed out the window.

The driver pulled out of the alley and into the street, racing forward as he and Tiao engaged in some kind of verbal feud.

"English?" I asked the driver.

Tiao replied, "Peng not speak English."

"Sure he does," I replied. "You and Cong speak excellent English, so I'm going to wager no expense was spared in your education. Peng included. You guys are all related, aren't you?"

No response.

We headed out of Lashio, quickly passing into the countryside. Vehicle traffic was interspersed with tiny motorbikes bearing multiple riders and pickups stacked high with crates, adults clinging to the moving cargo like lampreys on a whale shark, oblivious to the rain that fell steadily from cobalt clouds. Humped cattle moseyed at the ends of leashes held by genderless owners in ankle-length leg wraps, their faces shielded by straw rice hats. Then we passed a single-file row of civilians that stretched nearly a mile, their umbrellas bobbing in a solemn march.

"Funeral procession," Cong explained.

Suddenly the driver spoke. "You want English? I asked what in the fuck you are doing here. You were supposed to take refund and go. Not demand personal taxi to Laukkai. The Kokang people struggled long before you come, will struggle long after you go. You delay us by one day, but do nothing to help us. Or your item."

I leaned forward, trying to sound respectful. "Can you help me understand why the junta is defending the place with the item if their only intent is to burn it before they leave?"

"I see Cong did not explain. As anticipated. The junta did not invade Laukkai for holiday. Weeks ago they try to inspect our depot. Kokang fighters stopped them. Now junta is holding depot to send message. Not because of item."

"What do you mean, your depot?"

"Defended building. We protect shipments there. Drugs, guns, anything valuable to us."

I watched a cargo truck dwarfed by the load of soaked hay exploding out of its back, riders on the load and roof of the cab. "And the item is in this depot?"

"Yes. Most valuable thing there."

"You're sure it hasn't been destroyed yet?"

"It is hidden. In a marked box among many others. Routine shipment. I was on my way to recover, when junta invaded. Now depot is defended. Myanmar fighters will burn depot for same purpose as seizing it: to send message. Against Kokang for opposing the inspection."

Two huge passenger buses roared past at breakneck speed, both adorned in psychedelic color schemes. Peng swerved our car around a motorcycle riding low beneath long bundles strapped sideways and extending to the width of a truck.

"What kind of defenses does the junta have around the depot?"

"Enough to defend. Why you care?"

"We're stuck in a car together for five hours. It'll pass the time."

"The depot is on hill. They have cannon at top."

"Cannon?"

"Yes. Anti-aircraft."

"I doubt it's anti-aircraft, unless the Kokang have their own helicopters. Can you describe the weapon?"

Tiao stifled a laugh.

"Of course," Peng sneered. "Soviet S-60. Supplied by China. 57-millimeter round. Rate of fire 120 round per minute, cyclic. Accuracy is four thousand meters. And the cannon not for aircraft. Pointed downhill, so Kokang Army cannot approach it."

I sat back in my seat, astounded.

"Peng, you used to be in the junta, didn't you?"

"Ah," Tiao said, "you think, America? You sure?"

Peng answered, "Three years. Then bring training to Kokang Army. Tiao was five years, infantry. Cong"—Tiao interrupted him with a phrase in Chinese, to which Peng snickered before continuing—"Cong will go when he older. Tiao say, when his balls drop."

I nodded. "So that's how the Kokang Army learns how to fight. You send representatives to serve in the junta."

"Only a few. Chosen ones."

"But you know a hell of a lot about that S-60, don't you? What were you, air defense? Field artillery?"

"Air Defense. Eastern Sector. I have shot S-60. Many times. Seen what it does to target. So I know: Kokang Army not get depot back."

I thought about that for long minutes as I took in the terrain outside the window.

As we traveled northeast, jungled hills rose from rice paddies. Families and erratic clusters of children waved from roadsides bordered by telephone lines. Soon a placid river spread to our left, guarded by a jagged mountain beyond. The landscape became increasingly more desolate, the agricultural modifications erased as rice paddies gave way to scrub brush and endless rainy views devoid of people. The road threaded alongside a rugged cliff face.

Gone was the stunning tropical city and surrounding area teeming with brightly clothed civilians. A cargo truck rattled by, bullet holes between its headlights, the bed packed with people leaving our destination and, for all intents and purposes, quite happy to be doing so.

When buildings reappeared, they weren't the exquisitely adorned retail spaces of Lashio. Instead, we passed low-slung structures, brown and drab and dull, as if the architecture didn't want to call attention to itself. By the time I saw a few gloomy red roofs, they appeared almost psychedelic by comparison. A man and woman wandered along the trash-strewn streets carrying suitcases and bundles strapped to their backs, a small child following in their wake. We passed mud-covered streets, rickety gates, and construction additions made of sheet metal and plywood. A few billboards decked in Mandarin script and pictures of attractive women went unnoticed by the desolate streets. The few colored buildings in town appeared awkwardly painted and out of place.

Of course I was approaching a shithole, I mused. Like the other places I'd been, from Afghanistan to Iraq, Somalia to Brazil, I was seeing the paradox of a beautiful place ripped apart by war, where the civilians had either escaped or remained trapped, where tourists dared not tread. Only the shooters were left to experience the natural beauty of a landscape largely abandoned by those not seeking to kill. War didn't coincide with ugliness, it was the other way around—the most stunning of surroundings could be rendered horrid by combat, the natural world matching the ugliness of man blow-for-blow, calling the bluff of my species.

As the car neared Kokang my jet lag got the better of me. Lapsing into a fitful sleep, I had racing thoughts of the war in South America and my role in it, and the enemy leader who dared take on the Handler's organization. Then I saw another face—Agustin, the bearded man who'd drolly held an intimate and quasi-religious conversation with me as we observed the Christ the Redeemer statue in Rio, then personally led a kill team to hunt down Parvaneh and me in the favela.

It would be some time before I saw him again, I knew. But see him I would, after the Handler had been assassinated and Ian was free, and I was sent to join the war in South America. Once I found myself back on the same continent as Agustin, tasked with eliminating his organization, I'd make it my mission in life to personally hunt him down. I'd put a .454 revolver to his head and blow him away, just like I'd thought about doing to myself a million times in the past few years of my existence.

* * *

We approached the town of Laukkai at dusk.

Peng stopped the car at a turn in the mountain pass, glancing uphill as he flashed the high beams twice. From a cluster of trees atop the mountain to our left, a flashlight signaled five times in return.

We pulled forward again as Tiao made a call on his cell phone.

"Security is set," he said, hanging up. "We proceed."

Peng asked, "Which site?"

"Temple."

Peng muttered something that I took to be a curse in Chinese, then drove us another mile before stopping a final time.

We exited the car into a warm, muggy drizzle, my clothes immediately sticking to me with humidity. It felt smothering after my months in the crisp mountain heights of British Columbia. I thought back to that first freezing night in the cabin, hiding from a grizzly, amused at how far I'd come since then—literally and figuratively.

I followed the other three up a winding, crumbling trail toward a craggy rock face rising into a mountain above us.

Peng stopped me and pointed back the way we'd come. "That is Laukkai. The depot, on hill."

Through the fading light, I scanned an adjacent hilltop slightly higher than our current altitude that was marbled with swaths of buildings, roads, and footpaths. It was only two miles distant, if that, so close that despite Peng's warnings of the military defenses surrounding the depot, it felt like I could stroll up the hill and retrieve the item whenever I pleased.

Our trail ended at a set of stairs carved into the mountain, and we ascended them to a small, dark opening in the rock wall flanked by thin waterfalls splashing down the face. As we passed under a high red scroll marked with golden script, the rush of the waterfall receded into a swirling echo as we entered the mouth of a dimly lit cave.

The trio stopped abruptly, turning toward the staircase to stand watch.

Peng spoke to me in a low, monotone whisper. "You go alone. To end of cave. He will meet there."

"Who is 'he?'"

"The boss."

I nodded and took two steps into the cave before Tiao grabbed my shoulder and said, "No shoes."

"You're serious?"

He seemed to read my tone. "You give respect, America."

I stepped out of my shoes and, finding the ground to be a water-soaked slick of smooth rock, pulled off my socks as well before following a serpentine tunnel deeper into the mountain.

Periodic light bulbs glowed from a thin cord snaking across the jagged cave ceiling, shining dully upon intricate gold and white Buddha statues perched on every rock outcropping—hundreds of them spanning both sides of the wall as far as I could see, some small enough to hold in your palm and some larger than I was. Their serene expressions glowed among a universe of lit candles as they placidly watched me slip down the abandoned tunnel.

The rustle of my movements echoed between drips of water from above. Everything about the cave was a far cry from the muggy outdoors; the air inside was cool and clean, its own comfortable atmosphere alight with the smell of melted candle wax and wet rock.

Within minutes I reached a dead end, a final circular cavern whose walls were lined with more Buddha statues resting on rock outcroppings from floor to ceiling. Their shapes were cast in the pale glow of a final light bulb, and water dripped from the ceiling like a symphony of ticking clocks.

I whirled around at the sound of movement behind me, seeing a shadowy figure aiming a rifle at me while blocking the single path out. Where had he come from? There was zero chance that he'd followed me all that way unheard, but by the time this thought occurred I caught further movement in the cavern behind me.

Looking sideways, I glimpsed the shadows of the countless Buddha statues begin crawling across the walls, as if a single dark organism shifted around me. In the gloomy darkness I could discern men stepping out from behind the statues, rifles at the ready.

Did they send me here to be executed? Tiao might not have even spoken to the man in charge, or maybe he had, and I was being captured for ransom—or worse yet, sold to the Handler as a living conspirator long thought dead.

For endless seconds no one moved, least of all me.

Finally I said to no one in particular, "Surely you're not planning on damaging any of these statues with rifle fire. You guys trying to walk me out alive or what?"

No response. Dripping water, the guardians frozen against the walls around me.

"Anyone speak English?"

Another few seconds of quiet.

"How about Latin?"

An elderly voice rasped behind me, "My Latin is quite poor..."

I turned toward a giant Buddha at the end of the cavern as a shadow slipped out from behind it and approached me.

The shape passed under the muted glimmer of the lone light bulb and transformed into an old man, who finished, "...but my English? Passable."

He was barefoot too, walking lightly but with a slight hunch, hands clasped behind his back. As he stopped before me, I could see that he was bald, with a long face and bushy silver eyebrows slanted downward to the creases of his eyes.

A wave of relief overcame me. No kidnapping, this, nor an execution attempt—I'd just walked into a maelstrom of personal guards protecting someone very powerful.

I gave a respectful nod. "Thank you for coming, sir."

"My name is Kun. Not sir. Why have you come to this place, David?"

"As you know, there is an item in the Laukkai depot that I need."

"Not the item alone, then, but what I can make it."

"I don't follow."

"There are two parts to the item you seek. One is in my possession, the other is in the depot. Either on its own is quite useless to you."

"But once you combine them, they become invaluable?"

"Not invaluable: approximately 640,000 US. Subject to exchange rates, of course. That is the amount I am refunding the woman who sent you, with my deepest regrets. But I cannot alter the political course of my home-land, nor the military one, as my family has explained to you. On a personal note"—he leaned in toward me—"in over thirty years, I have never failed to deliver an order. It pains me to do so now. So please do not make me explain it again before you go."

I cleared my throat. "I didn't come here for you to explain it—I came for you to authorize a mission."

His low silver eyebrows began to rise with the hint of a smile. "My apologies, David. This meeting is done."

He turned to leave. Acting instinctively, before I had time to think better of it, I grabbed his arm to stop him.

The shuffle of footsteps exploded in the cavern as the black shapes of bodyguards moved toward me, then went silent as Kun raised his gnarled hand to wave them off.

I released him and he faced me once more, this time stepping closer, dark eyes boring into mine. "You have made a grave error coming here, David—"

"Hear me out," I said quickly, "please. I have an offer that serves us both."

"One minute. Then I leave."

"The woman who sent me will not take kindly to a refund. If she doesn't have the resources to rectify this breach of contract now, she soon will."

"I did not take you as the type to threaten, David."

"You are correct. What I'm offering isn't a threat, but a way to absolve yourself and your family of responsibility. She sent me as a full representative, yes?"

"Her ability to communicate is quite sporadic. So yes, she gave you authority to speak on her behalf. But that does not put you in a position to dictate orders."

"Of course not. What I'm recommending, with your permission and with all respect, is that you let me recover the component of my item that is currently being held in the depot."

"Quite impossible. The Kokang leader hides in the mountains. I cannot even reach him right now. The status of his counterattack is uncertain at present."

"You do not have to commit forces, merely authorize me to embark on a mission, on my own. If you can describe the item's exact location in the depot and provide me minimum armament—"

"My family has surely described the extent of junta defenses."

"And the fact that the Myanmar Army will burn the depot to the ground before they depart, yes." I nodded my concession to his point, then countered, "But with all respect, I believe your family underestimates what one man can accomplish against defenses that cannot conceive of such an audacious attempt."

Kun's brow furrowed, then relaxed. He seemed surprised at my proposal, but a tight smile preceded his next words. "So you act of your own accord, and the woman who sent you'will have no further basis on which to refuse a refund."

"Or cite a breach of contract. The Myanmar government took sudden actions beyond your control while I was on my way here, and I demanded to recover the item myself. She delegated authority to me, so any perceived blame no longer falls on you or your business. I will either succeed and recover the item and you keep your payment—"

"Or you will be killed, and the junta sets fire to our depot."

"In which case you send her a refund, as there is no item remaining to provide. She chose to send me, and she bears the consequences, good or bad."

He shook his head slowly. "What you propose is a bold move for one man when even the Kokang Army fears to attack the junta. My fear is that you are captured, then tortured and forced to reveal details of my network."

I swallowed and opened my mouth to speak, then hesitated. I would either convince Kun now or condemn Ian forever.

"What knowledge can I reveal?" I asked. "They must already know who you are, or you'd be traveling freely." I glanced toward the giant Buddha he'd emerged from behind. "A person of your stature wouldn't be meeting at a dead end. You've got the closest thing to becoming invisible: a hidden tunnel. But you've probably got a dozen other meeting sites that I don't know about. The safe house in Lashio is easily replaceable, and I know nothing of the men who brought me here besides a few first names and the fact that Peng and Tiao will probably celebrate if I get killed. This is worth the risk in order to preserve your reputation as a man who has accommodated client requests for thirty years. I won't let the junta break that record."

He remained silent at this, leaving us to the patter of water droplets from the cave ceiling. Then he replied, "Your chances are most doubtful."

"I will succeed."

"*If* you succeed, I believe it will be in a way neither of us expects. But"—he took a long breath—"I will allow you to try."

I felt like I'd been freed and sentenced to death in the same instant. "Thank you, Kun. I will see that—"

"Do not thank me yet, David. My people will give you what you need to embark. But now I must go. Nothing good results from remaining too long outside one's safe territory."

I smiled. "Story of my life."

With a rueful nod, Kun turned and disappeared behind the giant Buddha statue once more. The dark shapes of guards surrounding us converged into one amorphous shadow that slipped after him, leaving me alone.

9

Laukkai truly was a ghost town.

The only semblance of human presence I encountered on my journey toward the depot building was Myanmar soldiers. These were easy enough to spot—they were clustered in groups, their checkpoint locations chosen to shield warming fires from the steady pattering of rain, laughing and joking loudly as they passed the time. This much confirmed what I had hoped—the junta troops were expecting either a massive rebel counterattack or nothing at all. So long as the night was free of machinegun fire or rocket blasts, they probably felt as safe as if they were back on base.

I moved swiftly through the darkness, using a handheld night vision monocular to periodically scan my route. A silenced Makarov pistol was stuffed in my belt—holsters were apparently a luxury in this part of the world—and an AK-47 was slung tightly across my back. A single round from the unsuppressed assault rifle would announce my location to every soldier in the city, and its weight on my back represented little more than a last-ditch means to shoot my way out if cornered.

But it wouldn't come to that. The rain worked to my advantage as the defending troops tried to stay dry and warm, the sound of my movement concealed, the precipitation obscuring the view even if someone was looking for a single intruder. I was feeling light, stealthy, eager for the split-second judgment calls required in my immediate future. I'd throw myself into the situation and react on instinct, just as I had with my first assassination against Saamir. In his Chicago high rise, I'd been in a fight for my life against an armed guard force who knew I was in the building, with nothing but a silenced pistol and fewer magazines than I had now. And while I didn't have a getaway car waiting for me this time, I did have the added experience of dozens of firefights spanning the globe, most recently in Rio, where a gun and my instincts had prevailed, just as they always had. Just as they would tonight.

I weaved my way through the city with ease, circumnavigating the fires at Myanmar guard checkpoints, some so close that I could smell burning scrap wood and cigarette smoke even through the rain. Seemingly every civilian inhabitant had fled either deeper into Myanmar or into China through the border gate shortly beyond the hilltop I approached.

I stopped on a sloping dirt road and looked behind me at the jagged mountain marking the entrance to the Buddhist temple I'd flee to after getting what I came for. A massive, easily locatable terrain feature to help me navigate back. Turning to continue my infiltration route, I slipped down an alley and stopped at the corner to scan with my night vision, using the tip of my index finger to wipe the fog constantly accumulating on the lens.

The depot wasn't hard to find. It was seated prominently on the high ground, providing ample reason for the emplacement of the S-60 anti-aircraft gun. Scanning the hill with my night vision monocular, I could clearly make out the twin vertical armored plates protecting the gunner's seat, from which a fourteen-foot-long barrel pointed downhill.

Apart from the cannon, however, the Myanmar Army defended the depot by relying on manpower. Perhaps too much of it. The guard presence was spread among pre-established bunkers now fortified by piles of sandbags, and while this may have been sufficient given a properly motivated force equipped with night vision, it was almost counterproductive when staffed with low-ranking, ill-equipped junta troops.

I was reminded of invading Iraq with the Rangers. After parachuting in, we'd secured a desert landing site and landed transport aircraft with our mobility vehicles. Soon we were traveling by night, maneuvering our convoy to avoid fortified troop positions and Iraqi tank columns, any number of which could have destroyed us had they not failed to suspect the presence of an American raid force so far behind the front lines. I vividly recalled driving past an Iraqi anti-aircraft cannon firing skyward, its gunner completely unaware that less than three hundred meters away a convoy of Rangers was en route to a target. Hell, for all I knew he could have been shooting an S-60 just like the one guarding the hilltop I approached.

Limited guard forces made sentries more alert, compensating for their vulnerabilities; but a surplus of soldiers and deficit of fortified positions bred overconfidence, the unwarranted sense of assurance that *someone* would detect anything out of the ordinary. At the depot, that meant guards in positions I could spot under my night vision a hundred meters away, whose banter I could make out at half that distance.

Moving in a semicircle cloverleaf pattern around the depot, I probed for a gap in the defenses sufficient for a single man with night vision to slip through unnoticed. It took me less than two hours of close reconnaissance to confirm that my best route was along a divot of low ground between guard posts, cloaked in shadow.

The S-60 anti-aircraft gun watched the gap, making a daytime approach flat-out impossible; at night, however, I felt surreally confident. The cannon crew trusted the guard posts to spot minor threats in the night, while the guards trusted the men at the adjacent post to do the same. I lowered myself flat atop the slick, overgrown grass between buildings, the water oozing beneath my clothes amid the smell of wet, tropical earth. Pulling myself by my elbows, I writhed forward in a slithering high crawl that carried me through a channel of low ground between guard posts.

A chill began running through my core as I made steady progress forward. The journey would be infinitely more interesting on the way out, provided I wasn't running for my life with the missing component of Sage's item. It took me forty-five minutes to proceed less than a hundred meters uphill toward the depot, slipping between guard bunkers with the S-60 in full view ahead.

When I reached the depot, I stretched a hand to my side and touched the corner of the building—the cool, damp cinderblock wall felt welcoming, as if it had been waiting for me to arrive all along. Rising to a crouch, I followed the exterior wall toward a side entrance.

A sudden white light blinded me, followed by a half dozen more to my front and rear. Men screamed in Burmese as I instinctively went for my pistol. A rifle fired ten feet away—into the air, not into me—and I halted my pistol draw in place.

Armed men descended upon me, striking my body with rifle stocks and booted kicks. I went down and they grabbed me, stripping my weapons away in a few grunting, confused seconds while the rain pelted into me along with their strikes. I curled into the fetal position, unable to defend myself and overwhelmed by a sense of shame so profound that I almost didn't want to.

The violent assault was well deserved, an almost superficial abstraction weighed against my mental anguish in the moments of my capture. I was furious with myself more than with my attackers. I'd proceeded with an arrogant overconfidence that had served me before but had no place in Laukkai. By grossly underestimating the enemy, I'd just saved the Handler's life and quite likely ended my own.

And now, minutes before infiltrating my target building on a solo raid, I'd just become a prisoner of war in Myanmar.

DAMNED

Victoria aut mors

-Victory or death

10

The melee ceased long enough for someone to blindfold me and bind my wrists behind my back with a plastic cable tie. My equipment was ripped away, boots stripped off, and they executed a hasty pat-down search of my pockets. Now blind to my surroundings, I felt them drag me into the depot. I was overwhelmed with a sense of vertigo and panic as someone threw me backward, my shoulder blades striking a wall.

A sudden slap across my cheekbone dislodged my blindfold from one eye, revealing the blinding glare of flashlight beams directed at my face, ambient glimpses of men screaming, and rifles being pointed at my head. The smells of sweat and mildew, damp fatigues, and boot leather choked me as I squinted into the lights, looking away only to have them grab my jaw and force my face forward again. The screaming got louder, reaching some crescendo of fury that culminated in a rifle butt being thrust into my abdomen at maximum force. I fell to the floor, the wind gone from my lungs.

A man crouched beside me. "Where you from?"

I groaned, writhing in agony.

A gunshot exploded next to my face, so close that everything else vanished into the gonging sound erupting in my head. These men were crazy, reckless—they'd just discharged a weapon indoors, oblivious to or uncaring of the possibility of it ricocheting at themselves. A gun barrel was placed to my head, scalding metal burning my scalp.

The next scream from the man sounded distorted, warped, and muted even though he was next to me.

"WHERE YOU FROM?"

"America!" I shouted back. The heat of the barrel against my head disappeared as I panted for breath. A chorus of jeers from the men in the room, rollicking taunts in Burmese, another boot to my ribs.

This was a living nightmare—restrained, surrounded, encapsulated in a cell by men who wanted to torture or kill me, or both. No Outfit training scenario with a carefully scripted intervention, no one coming to rescue me. No one, in fact, who knew where I was beyond Kun and his men, who were now relocating any vestige of their network that had been witnessed by the foreigner who didn't return.

"I kill you now, America."

"No," I gasped, "please."

"Feed your body to dogs—"

A sudden barking shout silenced the entire room at once. I squinted upward, past the edge of my blindfold, and saw flashlights pointed at the ground, the men spreading to make room for a single man who entered through a lit doorway.

He began angrily screaming in Burmese, which sent the other men scurrying out the door.

"What have they done?" he asked, kneeling to set down a propane lantern. I rolled onto my side and he gently removed my blindfold, tossing it aside as I looked at his face.

He was too old to be a foot soldier—an officer, perhaps, though his mottled camouflage uniform bore no patches. He had a recessed hairline, his broad forehead catching a glimmer of the lantern beside him.

"I help you," he said, fumbling in his pocket and producing a small set of medical shears.

He leaned over me, sliding the rounded edge of a scissor blade against my wrist and slicing the cable tie. I brought my hands to my front, rubbing my wrists as my eyes adjusted to the light. The walls around me formed a windowless square, the single door now closed.

I took mental stock of my condition—I was bruised and beaten for sure, but didn't feel anything broken. Slowly I pushed myself upward to sit against the cinderblock wall as he stood. He was a slight man, just over five feet, and he pocketed the shears with an embarrassed shrug. "These men, they can be vigorous. Like all soldier. You good? Okay?"

I said nothing, looking at the ground, trying to remain non-confrontational. For all I knew, this guy was about to kick me in the face.

Then he declared, "I have other duty. You no talk to me, I leave. Soldier come back, ask you instead."

He picked up his lantern and turned toward the door.

"No." I shook my head. "Stay."

He set the lantern back down, watching me from his meager standing height. "Good. Cooperate, things well for you. Food. Water. Doctor."

I nodded slightly.

"My name Cetan. What your name?"

I responded instinctively, with the first name that came to mind. "Adam."

"Where you from, Adam? Tell, or I go now."

At some level I felt a deep, unbidden instinct to cooperate, to do anything that would improve my situation. The men outside were violent, and I was one misstep from broken bones at best and being shot at worst.

"America." I felt humiliated using the name of my country now that I was facing imprisonment or death as the result of my own hubris.

"Good. What you do here, Adam?"

A lump rose in my throat—what could I say? Cetan would catch me in a lie almost immediately.

"Adam. I ask you. What you do here?"

Before I could reply, he said, "You want water before speak?"

I nodded.

"Okay. Okay, Adam. I get you water."

Cetan picked up his lantern, then pounded three times on the door. After a pause it opened, and I caught a glimpse of the wall shortly beyond it as Cetan departed and it slammed shut again. There looked to be a hallway outside my cell—where in the depot did that put me? I pictured the diagram of the depot's layout that Kun's men had briefed me on, quickly realizing that I could have been in any one of half a dozen side rooms, all on the wrong side of the structure from my item.

I had a brief moment to observe the sickening irony of my situation— I'd ended up in the building I intended to infiltrate, but so hopelessly stranded from my goal that I may as well have never embarked to Myanmar at all. The room was warm with stale, tropical air, humid and unmoving in the space, and amid it my mind became a turbulent storm of converging emotions. One moment I felt deeply ashamed at being captured, deserving of any punishment that ensued, the next intensely vulnerable and fearful for my physical safety. A frantic desire to escape, mixed with the sheer helplessness at being unable to do so.

My pulse began to rise to a panicked state as my mind became gripped by sheer hysteria. Don't lose control, I thought. Focus. I shifted backward, felt my shoulder hit a wall, and sank against it. Sliding to the floor, I took long, measured breaths, forcing oxygen into my system until the pulse slamming in my brain began to quiet.

Control. Control. What next? Two options—death or escape. No one would come for me. But even as I acknowledged the need to escape at all costs, I couldn't begin to fathom how. There were no other prisoners, no distractions for my captors—my breath began to quicken again.

Don't think so far ahead, I thought. Make it one more breath, then two. Five breaths, then ten. You're David Rivers, I told myself, a whisper of mental strength returning. You've been through combat, bloodied but never broken. You'll find a way—you have to. For Ian. The only thing that can stop you is yourself. Karma's voice...*You know the only thing that's the end of the world, David? The end of the world. You can recover from everything else...*

The sharp creak of the door being thrown open was my only warning before thundering boots entered, flashlights shone in my face, and I was punched in the side of the head. Multiple men surrounded me, holding me down as the blindfold was put back on.

Then a gun barrel was pressed squarely to the center of my forehead.

"Do it," a man shouted. "Or die."

"What? Do what?"

The pressure of the barrel lifted.

"Stand."

I struggled to rise, bracing myself against the wall for support, but a sudden kick to my groin felled me in place with a scream of agony.

"I say *STAND!* You do fast!"

Grunting, I fought my way upward to a crouched position, the pain spreading from my testicles into my guts.

"Take clothes off."

"What?"

A hard backhand across my jaw, hot blood filling my mouth.

"Take clothes off. You touch blindfold, I kill."

I stripped off my shirt, dropping it to the floor beside me and facing the voice. A moment's hesitation before a sharp uppercut impacted my stomach.

"Take clothes *off!*"

I sucked in a breath and unfastened my pants, shucking them off my legs and peeling off my socks and boxers before he had a chance to hit me again. The sound of laughing and Burmese taunts filled the room. From what I could tell, at least five men were sharing the humor at my expense.

"You cold, America? No man, here."

More laughs. I said nothing.

Hands on my shoulders turned me in place, shoving me against the wall. They pulled my arms behind my back, slid the plastic loop of a new cable tie around both wrists, and cinched it so tight it cut off blood to my hands. Then they shoved me down onto a sitting position on the floor.

I heard a slosh of water just before a torrent of it splashed down over my head. Gasping, I heard the laughter roll backward out of the room, followed by the door slamming shut.

I began to shake almost immediately as the air temperature turned freezing with my abrupt soaking. Falling onto my side, I tried to force my butt over the cable tie to bring my hands to my front. My left arm surged with the same dazzling pain that had accompanied being shot months earlier, and I quickly realized that getting my restrained hands around my pelvis was impossible.

Struggling to my knees instead, I shuffled to a wall and smeared my face against the rough cinderblocks until my blindfold dislodged. Eventually I was able to get it off altogether, finding that the room was bathed in darkness but for a sliver of light at the entrance.

Pressing my back to the door, I probed its tinny surface with my fingertips but found no bolt or lock. Then I tested the handle, which held firm. I shivered with dampness, and briefly considered using my bare feet to locate my pants so I could contort my legs into them.

Instead I stepped sideways along the perimeter of my cell, feeling the wall with fingers beginning to tingle from lack of circulation. I had to find some sharp corner or edge to saw the cable tie against before my hands went completely numb.

But before I could, the door swung open.

Cetan entered with his lantern, pulling the door shut behind him. I turned to face my interrogator, naked but towering over him, knowing I could overpower and kill him before anyone could enter and stop me.

But enter they would, and I'd be executed in this fucking room.

My voice sounded low, angry as I spoke. "This is what you meant by water?"

"No, this not me." He set the lamp down and procured his medical shears. I turned away from him as he clipped the cable tie open and a rush of blood returned to my fingertips. I spun to see Cetan looking over my naked body as I found my boxers and pants, pulling them over my legs as he spoke.

"I see you have many scars. Do not make more. Now talk. What you do here, Adam?"

I had to tell him something—if he left empty-handed, my next beating was going to escalate to the point of permanent injury.

I slipped into my shirt before responding through my teeth, "America sent me."

"No. This lie."

"It's true. Contact my embassy. Tell them you found Adam."

"You lie me, I no stop soldier. They hurt you, you no speak."

Hell, I thought, if I was going to play an American agent I may as well act the part.

"No. Not anymore."

"No?"

"I'm an American named Adam." I made up a social security number, providing an old phone number minus the last two digits as Cetan struggled to document it on a notepad.

"Check with my embassy. They'll confirm my identity. If I am hurt any more, my government will not be happy and neither will yours. My country knows I'm in Laukkai and they'll be looking for me very soon. Contact my embassy and they will negotiate my return."

"We see. You tell truth, you get help. You lie...things not go well."

Cetan snatched his lamp, then pounded three times on the door. It opened a moment later, his lamp illuminating the far wall and projecting the shadows of other men before I was once again locked in.

The back of my neck burned with a mix of shame, guilt, and murderous rage. It would take them time to contact and receive a response from the US Embassy, time that I desperately needed to plan an escape.

Suddenly the door flung open, and a group of men flooded the room as one shouted, "Turn around!"

I did so immediately, facing the wall before I was roughly blindfolded. They spun me around, using a cable tie to bind my hands to my front this time—that much was an improvement. The tie was pulled snug but not constrictively tight. Someone tilted my chin upward, then placed a plastic cup to my lips.

I greedily drank as much water as I could, reveling in the refreshment to my parched throat. They finished pouring, and the final drops ran down my chin as they left the room, slamming the door behind them. A few sips of water, my reward for beginning to provide information.

I quickly rubbed my fingertips across the cell walls, feeling for anything sharp enough to saw my cable tie against. My mind boiled with the embarrassment of what everyone who'd ever doubted me would say if they ever found out about this jaunt—particularly Sage, who already thought I was just a trigger-puller surviving at the mercy of her strategic vision. I imagined her rage if she discovered I'd undertaken a disastrously impossible solo incursion.

And every member of my previous paramilitary team—Boss, Ophie, and especially Matz—would be rolling in their graves if they knew what I'd just done.

My stomach churned when Cetan came back much sooner than expected, the door locking behind him as he set his propane lamp down on the floor, his face lit from below.

He took out the medical shears, and I extended my wrists toward him. But he paused instead, placing the scissors back into his pocket. "No. You not cooperate. Your embassy say they never hear of you."

Had he called, or was he bluffing? Neither would have surprised me.

"That's impossible," I rasped. "Any duty officer there will be able to tell you."

Cetan shook his head gravely. "AK-47, a Makarov, night eye. Mercenary beard. You are no lost tourist. Maybe you think you helping freedom fighter? No freedom fighter here. The border states are corrupt. Kokang worst of all. Illegal casinos. Trafficking weapons, trafficking drugs. Fifty heroin refineries, Kokang alone. Trafficking human beings."

"I'm not trying to help anyone but my country."

"These soldier outside, they want kill you. Not me. You tell me one thing, I cut you deal. No prison. Home arrest in state facility. I only want know one thing: why you come here to depot? You tell whole truth now, I not ask again—"

The booming thunderclap of an explosion rattled the floor beneath me, and the light from his propane lamp flickered before resuming full strength.

Cetan jumped at the noise, his face assuming an expression of sudden terror—no dogged veteran of ground combat, this one. I heard the escalating reverberation of machineguns firing in bursts outside.

The rebel counterattack had begun.

Men began shouting in the hallway, followed by the receding thumps of their boots as they raced out of the building.

Cetan turned to pound on the door, but I slipped my arms over his head before he had time to finish raising his fist.

Pulling my wrists against his neck, I pinched his throat shut with the cable tie. Cetan's choking noises were lost in the gunfire as I maintained pressure until his entire body went limp.

I lowered him to the ground beside the lamp and released his throat before he suffocated to death—killing him wasn't worth the repercussions if I couldn't escape. I retrieved the medical shears from his pocket, hastily sliding the blunted tip of the blade between my wrist and the cable tie.

My fumbling hands lost control of the scissors, dropping them in the dim light. I mumbled a curse, frantically sweeping my fingertips across the floor until I found them. Then I forced myself to take a breath and focus intently. Placing my wrists beside the lamp, I maneuvered the scissor blades around the cable tie, then slipped my thumbs through the handles and squeezed to cut my restraint with a satisfying *clip*.

I dropped the scissors, desperately wanting to strip Cetan's uniform and don it in an effort to buy even a second's hesitation from any troops standing between me and safety. But his clothes were far too small for me, and the time required to make the switch too long—I had to exploit the confusion of the moment or I'd lose my sole fleeting advantage.

I ripped off Cetan's boots instead, stuffing my feet in—the boots were far too small, but cramped and uncomfortable footwear was better than being barefoot for what I was about to attempt. Quickly patting down his pockets, I found he'd brought nothing with him but the shears. I pounded on the door three times, exactly as Cetan had done when trying to exit. Unlike before, there was no immediate response—all or most of the junta soldiers had just run off to fight.

I checked the handle, finding it locked tight, and then knocked again as loudly as I could. A sudden earsplitting blast shook my room, followed by a second, then a third, the entire depot now reverberating—the S-60 anti-aircraft gun had opened fire outside. I pounded more frantically on the door.

As I was about to test my luck in kicking it, someone unlocked the door from the outside. I threw my full weight against it just as it started to crack open, bursting into the hallway expecting multiple guards—instead, there was only one left after the others ran off to fight. Not much taller than Cetan, he was scrambling to raise his rifle with a shout of alarm drowned out by cannon booms.

I tackled him with a visceral intensity, my body's entire adrenal supply coursing through my blood at once. Straddling his slight frame, I drove a fist across his face hard enough to scatter teeth with a spray of blood. Then

I grabbed his head with both hands and smashed it against the floor until he went unconscious.

Looking about like a startled animal, I saw a hallway that was empty in both directions. I stripped the guard's weapon—no wonder he couldn't shoot me in time. It was a hideous bullpup assault rifle, the selector awkwardly located on the left side of a buttstock from which a curved magazine extended. I slung it over my shoulder and dragged its owner's body into the room with Cetan.

The hallway was still empty, but that was a very temporary situation— clearly they'd left the most inept of their ranks to guard the locked cell door, but that would be remedied as soon as the surprise of the rebel counterattack wore off.

The S-60 fire dwarfed the sound of every machinegun, and for a brief moment I considered searching the depot for Sage's item.

But I realized that would be the worst decision I'd made since embarking on my solo mission. I was no longer a crusading warrior flinging myself into danger—my psyche was a fragile eggshell of its former self, I was starving, about to be hunted, driven to madness by lack of sleep and abject fear.

Unsure of my location in the building, and likely seconds from being discovered, I fled in the opposite direction of the gunfire, hoping to move away from enemy contact and therefore guard presence. I turned a corner and saw sunlight streaming in through a door left partially ajar. Beyond it I could hear the chatter of machineguns and deep *booms* of rockets impacting between blasts from the S-60 cannon, and it occurred to me that the last time I'd been so close to an anti-aircraft piece in action was as an invader of Iraq.

Now I was in Myanmar, this time as an evader.

I burst outside into the morning sunlight amid the clashing thunder of war, the sounds a legitimate cause for terror for most, but in that moment they were a sweet, blissful symphony reverberating in my ears, the very sound of freedom.

I looked downhill, seeing two guard bunkers trading shots with rebel fighters in the city. None of the junta soldiers were watching the depot to their rear. I charged between them and into the mass of buildings beyond, adrenaline fueling my pumping legs into the fastest sprint I'd ever managed. A few potshots impacted the wall beside me, but I paid them no mind—I was moving dangerously, recklessly fast now, past one building, then across a street toward another, down an alley, vaulting abandoned bicycles and piles of brick like an Olympic steeplechase champion, moving ninety degrees from the audible shooting.

The entire city was abandoned save military units clashing with the rebels, and this left me a wide berth to make good on my escape. My confidence surged back in full force. I was certain that I wouldn't trip or make the slightest misstep, certain I could run the two miles back to the cave and have plenty of fuel in the tank to continue beyond that if needed.

And I was right.

Gradually I located the jagged mountaintop I'd departed from the night before, and threaded my way toward it as explosions and gunfire rocked the once quiet town of Laukkai.

11

I was escorted from a panel van into a building—quickly, so I wouldn't see my surroundings in detail. I'd been kept in the back of the van during the ride from the shrine to our present location, so I truly had no idea where we were.

And I didn't care.

The floor of the room I entered was lined with pillows, and Tiao directed me to sit as he and Peng joined me in a circle. Kun entered with the same elderly shuffle I'd first seen when he emerged from the shadows of the temple, and he slowly took a seat across from me with assistance from his grandson Cong.

Tiao began, "Car ready to take America back—"

Kun silenced him with a hand and then spoke in Chinese to Cong, who bowed and left the room.

Turning his face to Tiao, Peng, and me in succession, Kun spoke at last. "David, please explain what happened."

I looked up at the late morning sunlight spilling through the window, casting glowing beams filled with sparkling dust particles.

"I was a guest of the junta overnight. Fairly gracious hosts, as military interrogators go."

Peng huffed a sigh of indignation.

Kun raised a gnarled finger toward me. "What did you say of my network?"

"Not a word. I gave them a false name, false identification number, told them to contact the US Embassy for an explanation. I was able to escape during the confusion of the rebel counterattack."

He lowered his hand to his lap, closing his eyes. "I hope for your sake that you are not lying. As we speak, my sources are obtaining the junta's report of your interrogation."

I could only nod, letting the words—and the threat they thinly veiled—pass before responding. "I'm certain of your ability to learn what occurred during my interrogation. Trust that if I betrayed you, Kun, I would not have returned to your protection. My presence here speaks to the fact that I'm telling you the truth—and that I wish to discuss another option."

"I fear that all options, David, are quite exhausted."

"Most options, yes. But not all—I'm still a surviving agent."

"Of a woman who cannot yet be contacted."

"Therefore I still have full authority to negotiate on her behalf."

Tiao interjected, "*Had* full authority. Proper English. Past tense. You fail. Now you go."

Peng nodded his agreement. "Kokang counterattack failed. They have many casualties. Asked Wa Army to bring two thousand men, but they not arrive until tomorrow."

I seized on this new information. "If the Kokang and Wa armies make a combined attack on the junta tomorrow, that's the perfect time to recover the item. I was in that building and saw the confusion that ensued during the counterattack this morning. With two thousand more troops, the junta won't be able to hold the depot."

"If in danger," Peng replied sadly, "junta will call airstrikes. Perhaps win. Perhaps not. But fighting will get worse. If Kokang and Wa armies lose, we have no home. Kun, we should leave now. Return only if our armies win. Not remain to plan next failure. Not endanger the family."

Kun's eyes opened at this last word.

"Where is your family?" I asked.

Tiao glowered at me. "Not your problem, America."

"Sure it is. They're not here, are they? You're mentioning family, but if they were in immediate danger you'd have left already. You want to keep them safe? That means no one in North America blaming you for a breach of contract, no chance that they try to find you to right a wrong."

"This threat?"

"There's no threat here, I just—"

"Arrogance," Tiao shouted. "We give refund, you want talk boss. We drive Kokang, you want mission. You fail—"

Peng interrupted, "If Kokang Army did not attack, you be on way to Insein Prison. Right now."

I opened my mouth to respond when Cong entered the room holding a steel tray with a teapot and cups. Kneeling, he filled four cups and handed them to us, starting with Kun.

Finally I replied, "If you think prison is bad, you have no idea what kind of people I work with. They are beyond ruthless—women, children, nothing is sacred. I tried to assume the risk so none of you would have to, and I failed." I looked to Kun. "Now I'm asking for your help."

Peng gave a short laugh, but fell momentarily silent under Tiao's irate stare. Then Peng accused, "Your employer so ruthless, why you pretend to care about us?"

"I have no other choice." I looked to Kun again. "I am desperate."

Cong made a move to sit, stopping upon a quick stream of Chinese from Kun. After pausing to look at me, Cong turned and left the room.

Directing my gaze back to Peng, I continued, "I'm not trying to endanger your family, I'm trying to keep them safe. My goals and yours are served by my return with the item. I'm not telling you to remain here until the Kokang Army succeeds or fails—I'm telling you to give me one more day. And some men. Kun, with all respect, the reasons you authorized my mission in the first place still apply. Only one thing has changed: the tactics we use to recover the item."

Tiao hissed, "Not 'we,' America. *You*. One chance. You fail."

Kun spoke at last. "David, what do you propose?"

I spun my teacup in my hand, the heat of the tea scorching me through the porcelain.

"That we plan another mission."

"Plan?" Tiao shook his head. "Your face broken. By junta. In depot."

Peng leaned forward and stabbed a finger at me. "You failed, now you want us do work. For you."

"Not for me. *With* me."

Tiao shook his head briskly, his face reddening. "Now you want go back depot. Of course. With us protect you."

"You won't be protecting me. You'd be following me, because I'd be leading the mission."

Peng shouted, "You think you *lead* us? This is not your home. This is our fight."

"When the bullets are flying," I corrected him, "it's everyone's fight."

I watched Kun's elderly face brimming with some unseen emotion—frustration? Outrage? I turned to him.

"Kun, in the temple you said that if I succeeded, it would be in a way neither of us expected. Let me prove you right."

Peng chuckled to himself and then took a sip of tea. A slight smile played on his lips as he retorted, "If we go near depot, the cannon *will* destroy us. No question."

Kun made a clucking sound with his tongue. "I will hear David's plan."

With that, all eyes in the room swung to me: Kun's expression curious, Peng's bearing a petulant undertow of irritation, and Tiao's now bordering on fury.

"It must be *our* plan, not mine," I began carefully, "because all of you know this land better than I ever could. We've now seen what kind of trouble one overconfident American can get into, so let's figure this out together. There is only one approach to the depot—up the hill, in the sights of the anti-aircraft gun. Can we get a sniper to take out the S-60 team?"

Peng shook his head resolutely. "Fortified positions. High ground. S-60 gunner behind armored plates."

"Then we'll eliminate the S-60 altogether."

"Our rockets not so accurate. Not at this distance."

"Mortars?"

"Again. Not accurate enough. If they go through roof, could destroy item."

Tiao confirmed, "Peng right. We wait for junta to burn depot. Then, look for item."

"This the only way," Peng agreed. "We search remains of depot after fire."

"That's it," I gasped. "Fire."

Tiao nodded, thinking I was agreeing with him.

"No, I don't mean we let the depot burn. In America we have a saying, 'Fight fire with fire.' If we can't take out the S-60 by any other means, then we destroy it with something just as powerful."

Peng frowned, setting down his cup. "No cannons in Kokang. Not even good mortars."

"Because you're the smallest ethnic army." I looked from him to Kun. "That's why the junta is picking a fight with your slice of the region first, right? To destabilize the border groups by attacking the easiest target. But you've got an alliance with the Wa Army—two thousand fighters coming, right? Have they got a cannon, Peng?"

He considered the question. "Yes. A ZPU-1."

"Good, we'll have them position it to fire on the depot. Take out the S-60, then blow a hole in the side of the depot, opposite the item. I'll take a team inside."

"Junta counterattack would destroy us."

"If we stay in place," I agreed, "but that's not what we're going to do. Let's say we get in. Tiao, you used to be junta infantry. How many men to hold off a counterattack for a short time, until we can retrieve the item?"

"Twenty, thirty."

"Let's call it twenty. And I'll need ten inside the depot to clear out any resistance."

Tiao shook his head. "Thirty men, get seen. Get shot."

"We'll stage close, wait for the Wa Army's cannon to take out the S-60. First shot is our trigger to move; as we advance up the hill without the risk of S-60 fire, the Wa Army's anti-aircraft piece fires into the depot wall. Breach is clear as we reach the building; I take a ten-man raiding team inside, the other twenty set up blocking positions to prevent Burmese reinforcements from getting to us until the item is recovered. And as soon as we escape, the Wa Army can fight the junta counterattack. They give us a few shots from their cannon, we give them all the Myanmar Army soldiers they care to kill. At least until any airstrikes arrive."

No immediate rebuttal from any of the three men. I decided to press the advantage.

"This serves every party—it degrades junta forces, strengthens the alliance between the Kokang and the Wa armies, and allows us to get our item. There is risk, yes, but it delays your departure to safe territory by only a day. It allows you to deliver on your promise to my employer. And even if we fail to get the item, this plan ensures long-term protection for your family because you've taken every possible measure to fulfill your contract. Kun"—I looked at him expectantly—"this is the best plan we're going to get."

Kun didn't immediately answer, or even appear to be interested. Instead his eyes fluttered toward the ceiling, dancing amid the flecks of sunlit dust floating in the air above us. Tiao and Peng waited, the silence hanging heavy.

At last Kun said raspily, "If the Kokang Army will contribute the required men, and the Wa Army their cannon, then I will approve this operation."

Peng was expressionless, merely raising his tea cup to take another sip. Tiao looked frustrated that he hadn't dissuaded Kun, but beneath it I could see something else—a ripple of excitement, of eager anticipation. He was looking forward to a fight.

"Thank you, Kun," I said, feeling my shoulders relax as I breathed a heavy sigh of relief. "When can we get confirmation from the ethnic armies?"

"I can have a Kokang lieutenant here before sunset. His name is Zixin."

* * *

Zixin strode in the door two hours later, a squat predator in black street clothes. His eyes were narrow and wide-set, and he carried himself with an alert posture and visibly military bearing. I smiled at the sight of him. Kun followed just behind, looking mournful, though I couldn't imagine why. Zixin appeared more brash general than young lieutenant, and if he was the leader of our twenty-man perimeter security, then we were in good shape.

I approached Zixin, appreciating his muscular bulk all the more upon realizing he was close to a foot shorter than me. He shook my hand firmly, easily.

"Mr. David. A pleasure." Heavily accented English, without the extent of the education that had polished Peng, Tiao, and Cong.

"Thank you for coming, Zixin. Has Kun spoken to you about the plan?"

"Yes." He nodded sharply. "I get twenty men."

"Wonderful."

"Except—"

"I'll take Tiao, Peng, and Cong on the raiding force along with four of your men, leaving sixteen for perimeter security. We can make do with that."

"Mr. David, mission cancel."

"What do you mean?"

"Wa Army retreat," he explained. "One hour ago."

I almost gasped. Victory was so close at hand.

Zixin continued, "Border alliance now broken. Sorry, Mr. David."

I looked to Kun. "Get their cannon up here."

"They will not—"

"320,000 US dollars says they will. Split my employer's refund—you get half instead of nothing, they get the other half in exchange for one cannon with crew."

Kun shook his head sadly. "You do not understand; this is a political decision. The junta has negotiated safety of the Wa region in exchange for success of their Kokang offensive. The Wa leadership will not endanger their people in exchange for money. China would double your proposed payment to maintain border stability, and do so without hesitation."

"Hire the cannon crew as mercenaries, then. We are one anti-aircraft gun away from victory here."

"This is impossible. The ethnic armies may betray one another, but never their own blood. This is not how things work here. There will be no cannon. We are done."

I blurted, "There are no impossible odds, only lacking imaginations."

Kun shuddered with distaste, extending an upturned palm toward me. "If our imaginations are lacking, then please...enlighten us."

I closed my eyes in frustration, a blitzkrieg exploding in my mind.

The hopeless futility of it all—months of rehabilitation and solitude, an unimaginable opportunity to seize everything I wanted, only to find a military intervention in progress. Ian in captivity, and the entire universe conspiring against my every effort to bend the world to my will, to slay the Handler, who sat godlike atop a throne of human carnage. Sage holding the knife to my throat in the cabin—

"David."

Focus. None of that mattered right now. The item in the depot, the depot defended by the Myanmar Army. At least twenty defenders on site, but they'd be able to reinforce quickly from other defensive positions in Laukkai. An anti-aircraft gun keeping watch from the hilltop, and my mind's ability to formulate a plan in the next sixty seconds would either redeem Ian and me, or condemn us both.

Sage's voice: *You're a shooter, not a strategist.*

"Mr. David," Zixin said impatiently.

I'd never planned a real military mission—not as a young Ranger private, certainly not as a West Point cadet discharged before infantry officer training. But I'd been on so many raids in training and combat, both military and criminal—and I'd seen the depot up close and in person. I mentally reviewed the terrain and approaches around the building, snapshots of my infiltration and escape flashing through my mind in rapid succession. Tiao, Peng, and Cong speaking English, Zixin as a Kokang Army lieutenant with twenty men. No means to eliminate the anti-aircraft crew with sniper, mortar, or another cannon; no means to approach undetected in daylight; not enough night vision to conduct such a large mission after sunset. A rebel counterattack in progress—

"David!" Kun shouted.

Cetan taunting me. The pleasure in choking him. Stripping off his boots to make my escape—

My eyes burst open. "I've got it!"

The ambient light in the room seemed blinding, like I was waking from a drunken blackout, then my vision cleared and I saw both Zixin and Kun looking at me strangely.

I pointed at Kun. "You've got a hand in everything illegal going on in

Kokang. Drugs, guns, and humans require an extensive smuggling network, one that runs throughout the country."

"What is your point?"

"Myanmar Army uniforms!"

He shrugged absently. "So? What about them?"

"You must have some on hand," I continued. "Probably police uniforms and passports, too, but we don't need those. We need Myanmar Army uniforms. Enough for Zixin's blocking force and the raiding party, so twenty-five or thirty should do it."

Kun lowered his chin, flashing me a look of disappointment. "David, these uniforms are not easy to come by. We may have six or eight here, but that is it. To get more requires a purchase from my contacts in Napidaw, maybe three days to arrive."

"No time—they could burn the depot any day now, and probably would have already if the Kokang Army hadn't counterattacked. We have no time to spare. However many uniforms you have, that's the size of our raiding party."

Zixin grunted, "This does not solve problem."

I threw my arms up. "Don't you get it? We don't hide the raid force from the Myanmar Army, we present it to them. We approach uphill in broad daylight, pretend to be a junta squad with a broken radio. They won't risk shooting their own troops, and they won't know we're imposters until we're close enough to take out the guards—and seize the S-60."

Kun spoke quickly. "Then perimeter security moves in—"

"And since Peng knows how to shoot the S-60, he uses it to blow a hole in the depot. I take the raiding party inside, and we fight our way to the item. Everything else is according to the original plan. Forget the Wa Army, we don't need them—this is how we do this operation, right now, with the resources we've got."

Zixin looked confused, unable to follow the rapid-fire English between Kun and me. Kun then spoke to him in Chinese, and Zixin's wide-set eyes creased with recognition.

He gave as much of a smile as he was capable of—in his case, a muted slant of his mouth. "Might work."

"No, it *will* work." My pulse was quickening, hands gesturing excitedly.

"And when it does, it will elevate the fame of the Kokang Army. The raiders will be heroes to the Kokang people." I glanced from Zixin to Kun. "This victory will cement your reputation with international criminal networks and secure your legacy for another decade of business. We'll need to start rounding everyone up, and move as soon as possible."

Kun pressed a hand to my shoulder. "You are forgetting one thing."

"What? We've got the men, the plan, the uniforms and weapons, and the balls to pull it off. That's all we need."

"The raid will occur in daylight, yes? And you will move with the men in Myanmar Army uniforms?"

"Absolutely. I'll stay near the back until we're close enough for them to see I'm white anyway. What am I forgetting?"

His expression lightened with amusement. "Your beard, David. This is visible at great distance. It will have to go away."

I half chuckled, taken aback at this grievous oversight, as Kun continued, "I have some stolen straight razors from China. Do you know how to use one?"

"Of course." I slapped him on the arm. "I'm a former prisoner of war, not a complete failure."

* * *

I stared at the face in the mirror—at the deep green, unflinching eyes; at my long, dark blond hair roughly combed back; at the coarse beard clinging to my face. In that moment, I thought of my exile in the Dominican Republic—stranded in the safe house, drinking and writing the story of my time with Boss's team. Back then I'd come to the bathroom mirror to stare at myself as I played Russian roulette with my .454 revolver, watching the dancing green eyes in the mirror, reveling in the burst of guilty adrenaline that flushed into my bloodstream with every empty click of the chamber.

Beads of water clung to my facial hair like dew. How long had it been since my father taught me to use a straight razor? I was still a teenager then, long before the military had necessitated rushed pre-sunrise shaves with cartridge razors and canned foam.

What was I becoming? A purple ring lined my blackened right eye, my cheekbones were mottled with bruises, my lip was split by the junta assault, the bridge of my nose bore the red slash of torn skin. My eyes were the same, yet different somehow—less impulsive and more calculated, colored with the things I had seen in Somalia and Brazil, reflecting a grim determination to succeed in freeing Ian at all costs. Since my journey of vengeance had begun, I'd met the Handler, stared into his amber eyes, smuggled in a gun to attempt his assassination. An intervention by Sage, followed by months in the wilderness watching eagles glide on thermals high above the pine trees, snow-capped mountains in the distance, alone with a mind that had turned from enemy to ally, from self-destruction to salvation.

There was no badger brush or shave cream here; instead, I used a half-bar of soap to hand lather a mass of suds, rubbing them into my beard with my fingertips.

I'd gone after the item in the depot by myself, the sum total of my willpower, experience, instincts coming up inadequate. I'd gone as far as I could as a lone operator; now I needed to become something more. I would not fail again. Even if I sacrificed myself in the mission, I would ensure the item made its way back to Sage, that it succeeded in its intended purpose. In the past I'd failed everyone close to me: Karma, Boss's team, even Parvaneh, though she alone had lived to resent me for it. Ian was the only person left to save, my final chance at redemption.

Continuing to rub the milky white soap in circular motions on my cheeks and jaw, I worked a dense foamy lather over my beard, massaging it under the whiskers.

What was I becoming? There were times when this journey seemed an immovably dense mass of depression and anguish, others when it was an incredibly fast-paced adventure. Traveling the world and battling men no different than me, seeing who would emerge from the gunfight with their lives to show for it.

Wheeling open the straight razor, I lightly brushed my thumb across the fin of the blade from bottom to top; it was usably crisp, a mass-produced Chinese blade of decent quality mounted onto a wobbly plastic handle. I'd probably become a blood donor on this passage, but the beard had to go. Compared with the likelihood of getting shot in the upcoming raid, I could tolerate a few more facial cuts.

Twisting the straight razor open at a reverse ninety-degree angle, I reached over my head to pull my sideburn taut. Wincing as tender skin was pulled tight, I touched the blade to the edge of the cream, then began short, feather-pressure strokes downward with the grain of my hair. The whiskers popped off with a crisp whisking sound, and I worked halfway across my face before switching the razor to my opposite hand and resuming.

Yet now things were different than any mission I'd ever conducted as a soldier or mercenary; now I'd been granted other fighters under my command. I'd long been flippant toward the prospect of my own death. But losing a man due to my own decisions, or lack thereof, would certainly follow me until the day I died. Was I ready for that possibility?

My thoughts were interrupted by the sight of my ridiculous-looking face in the mirror. Contrary to the movies, true straight razor shaving involves a choreographed sequence of pulling on your cheeks, followed by exaggerated expressions to draw the skin taut, and then passing over the whiskers a blade sharp enough to slash a man's throat. The more ridiculous you look, my father had assured me, the less blood you'll spill. He'd regarded disposable cartridge razors as a pitiable concession to the ranks of men working miserable day jobs until they died; the men destined for greatness, he said, were "wet shavers." Brush and blade—straight razor or double-edged, it didn't matter—making their own lather and executing a shave with focus lest the slightest distraction scar them for life.

Why had I stopped shaving like this? What other lessons had I forgotten from my father, to this day my only true guiding light?

During my first shaving pass, I moved the razor with the grain of my hair. Now I re-lathered and ran the blade perpendicular to the grain, coming one degree closer to smooth skin. No blood. Then I began a third pass, sliding the razor against the grain in the most difficult of techniques.

I didn't feel like a leader. I felt equal parts total imposter and debutante, both fated and impossibly unsuited for the task I had been dealt.

So what would I do?

I would execute. Even if I died, even if everyone under my command did, there was one fate worse: to know that Ian was alive, enslaved, and I had done less than I was capable of to free him.

I washed the excess soap lather from my face, seeing newly exposed skin free of stubble, impeccably smooth and without a single weeping drop of blood to show for it.

12

There were eight of us in the raiding party, our number dictated by how many Myanmar Army uniforms Kun had on hand. Myself, Tiao, Peng, and Cong made up half the team. The other four were Kokang fighters purported to have combat experience. None spoke English.

Zixin's perimeter security had reached its staging area as my raiding party moved quickly uphill and between buildings amid rainfall that was sparse and stinging yet fell from a ceiling of turbulent charcoal clouds. Above the sound of rain we heard periodic gunfire and explosions on the town's periphery. The Kokang Army had sought refuge in the wild green hills surrounding the village, using the jungle to move large formations of men toward clashes with junta outposts. It was the perfect distraction to allow the eight of us in uniform to slip through the village toward the depot —while we wouldn't fool anyone up close, particularly with my complexion, at a distance we were passable as a junta squad moving to reinforce another position against the rebel attacks.

Tiao had identified the rifle I'd stolen from the depot guard as a Chinese Type 95, commonly enough available elsewhere that we'd been able to outfit the raiding party with them. We also had pistols tucked into our belts. My handgun was a suppressed Indian 9mm automatic that I carried for sentry disposal: the more stealthily we could remove perimeter guards, the closer we could get to our target building before being compromised.

As we closed in on the depot, I could tell Tiao was good in a fight—he moved confidently, alertly, carried himself in a way that couldn't be faked when enemy contact was imminent. Peng appeared less certain, though that much was understandable given he was an air defense soldier by training, not a ground fighter. Cong, by contrast, was doing his best to appear brave yet looked like he'd borrowed his father's uniform to play soldier for a day. The four militia members were casual enough about the entire affair that I knew they'd happily followed orders a great deal in the past, though whether they were good in a fight remained to be seen.

We took a circuitous route toward the depot, keeping ourselves in relatively low ground as long as we could to avoid being spotted.

As we reached the bottom of the hill, the rainfall increased to a steadier pattering. Tiao spoke over it to address me.

"This it, America. You ready rock and roll?"

I mustered a grin. "Ready when you are, Tiao."

He glanced to Peng, then tipped his head toward me. "Hide the roundeye."

"I don't really want to be spoken to like that, you racist..."

But Tiao was already bounding ahead of our group, helplessly waving his radio over his head and shouting to the guards in Burmese. Peng and the others clustered in front of me as we walked up the hill, weapons slung casually over our shoulders.

One guard had risen from the bunker to respond to Tiao, and I could see another rising to a knee to look at us, the hood of a slick green poncho over his head. These were foot soldiers, complete privates, left to stand guard in the rain in a position where rebel infiltration was least likely.

Tiao came to a stop, articulating wildly as he spoke and subtly maneuvering himself to leave me a clear line of sight to the standing guard. The guard was laughing at Tiao's banter as the rest of us closed in, and once we were within ten feet I made my move.

I pushed Peng aside with one hand, stepping forward and leveling the suppressed pistol at the guard kneeling in the bunker. Two of the fastest shots I've ever taken, first at the kneeling guard and then the standing, both hits. *Tick, tick*.

Tiao was pulling his rifle to a firing position before the bodies had fallen—there must have been a third guard in the bunker—and I ran alongside it to take a suppressed shot before rifle fire compromised us.

It was too late.

A blast of flame from Tiao's barrel, and the shots echoed over the rain, over the distant gunfire, over the entire village.

We took return fire from the soldiers uphill almost immediately, the guards around the anti-aircraft piece engaging us with assault rifles as their rounds kicked up mud around us. Our group had just begun firing back when we were attacked from behind—and, turning, I saw a formation of Myanmar soldiers starting to maneuver toward us from below.

We were never going to make it to the cannon as a single team.

Peng was the only one who could fire the anti-aircraft gun, and Tiao was the most experienced fighter. We had barely enough augmenting Kokang troops to help them overtake the cannon, and since they didn't speak English they were of little use to me at present.

I grabbed Cong's rain-soaked sleeve and shouted, "Cong and I will hold them back until Zixin's men arrive. Get the cannon."

Tiao didn't hesitate and neither did I—by the time I readied my radio, his six-man element was vanishing over the hill.

I keyed the mic and said, "Perimeter security, now!"

Zixin's voice responded, "*Yes*."

Cong was standing in the open, wild-eyed.

"Get over here!" I yelled.

He crouched next to me.

"Not *next* to me! Get over to the other side of the bunker!"

He scrambled to the opposite corner at once, calling back, "What now?"

I pulled every Type 95 magazine from the chest racks of the three dead guards, splitting them between myself and Cong. I anticipated that we wouldn't make it out of this scuffle with less than ninety rounds per man being fired.

This would quickly turn out to be a gross underestimate.

I looked down the barrel of my rifle, watching for the first enemy fighters to appear. "Put your rifle on single shot," I told Cong. "When you see those Myanmar troops coming up the hill, start lighting 'em up. Two shots per man, then move to the next. You work right to left, I work left to right."

Automatic weapons fire continued behind us, and I had to force myself to keep my focus downhill—if Tiao and his element didn't succeed in over-running the cannon, then we were all dead anyway.

I keyed my radio again. "Zixin! Get your men here now!"

"*I hear you.*"

Cong asked, "What else?"

"Nothing, man. Just enjoy yourself. Shooting people is the most fun you can have with your clothes on—"

I fired twice as a man's silhouette appeared over the crest to my front before immediately dropping with a puff of smoke.

Cong began firing wildly, and I shouted at him.

"Two shots per man, Cong! Stop wasting ammo."

"I have many magazines—"

"So do I. But we might need them all."

More human silhouettes appeared—at the divots of the hill, and at the corners of buildings. I was engaging soldiers as fast as I could see their murky figures through the rain, and failing pitifully to keep up with new targets. Crevices of the landscape, bathed in shadow, were illuminated with the flash of weapons firing toward us.

Rounds slapped against the front of the bunker, popping into the sand-bags above us, occasionally cracking through the air beside my head. These guys weren't elite fighters, but they weren't exactly basic trainees either. While their marksmanship wasn't incredibly accurate, I'd hoped to hear wild bursts of rifles on full auto rather than the disciplined shots impacting around us.

Cong's rifle barked consistently, reassuringly, as he mirrored my efforts on the opposite side of the bunker. Enemy fighters were bounding from building to building toward us, taking up new shooting positions quicker than I could locate them. By the time I'd suppressed one junta soldier, two or three more had appeared and opened fire on us. Our efforts were a very temporary reprieve against the Myanmar soldiers fighting their way to the depot, and we desperately needed to be reinforced by Zixin and his perimeter security force.

I loaded my last magazine.

Cong shouted, "They will run over us!"

"If we're killed, we've got nothing to worry about. Give me a magazine!"

He tossed one my way, and I had to reload in the span of forty seconds of shooting. I'd likely only scored a few lucky kill shots. The two of us couldn't shoot men fast enough, and the assaulting force had become well aware of this.

"Another magazine!" I called.

"No more," Cong shouted back. "I am out."

I drew my pistol, unscrewing the warm suppressor as fighters started to spill onto the hillside. They were charging forward because our rifle fire had ended, and it was better they hear my pistol shots than nothing at all.

Feeling ludicrously inadequate, I began popping single handgun rounds at the front runners of a formation racing toward us like a Civil War reenactment. They feared their leaders' orders more than us, and we didn't have the ammunition or the numbers to reverse that equation. I wanted to run but realized at once that if we broke contact and fled toward Tiao, we'd be killed crossing the open ground to our rear.

I spoke into my radio. "Zixin, we need your men here!"

Zixin's disjointed voice streamed from the radio. "*We having difficulty.*"

"Get up here right now, or Cong and I are dead."

"*I am trying.*"

I wanted to beeline to Zixin's position, leaving the mission and my item behind just to kill him. We both knew his men had been staged before the raiding party approached the hilltop. He was hedging his bets: if we failed to make entry, he'd retreat with the lukewarm excuse of something beyond his control. If and when we breached the depot wall, he'd come racing in, guns blazing, to capture some of the glory.

Cong shouted at me, "What now?"

I squeezed off three more pistol rounds at the marauding junta soldiers.

"Die in place," I called back. At some level I knew he'd panic and flee, and wouldn't make it more than three steps before being gunned down in the mud.

But instead I heard the *pop pop* of Cong's pistol as he remained in the fight, same as I did. I wanted to smile and cry at the same time—the kid had guts, had potential, would've made a fine fighter if he didn't have to die out here in pursuit of some unknown item, another life lost in the effort to unseat the Handler's regime. I kept shooting, but there must have been two dozen junta soldiers and only ten seconds until they were upon us.

I reloaded my pistol and had just continued firing when the hand of God wiped our enemy from the face of the earth.

A wall of blood and earth and smoke, limbs flying and a torso with one arm spinning in a high arc over the crowd as 57mm rounds from the S-60 anti-aircraft cannon did to fragile human bodies what they had been designed to do to helicopters.

The roar of each shot sucked the air from my lungs. Scalding hot wind coursed over us in a fiery tempest, the reverberating shots splitting time and space in a series of otherworldly blasts.

I put my head down, trying to sink as low as possible into the ground, and covered my ears until I realized the shooting wasn't about to stop. Glancing up, I saw that Peng was going full cyclic, sending massive super-sonic rounds into the hillside and every building that once hosted Myanmar Army fighters.

The cannon eviscerated formerly stoic buildings, and explosions of cinderblock and brick swept back and forth until all resistance had ended. There was no one left to kill, or at least no one willing to fight, after Peng's melee. After the first continuous seconds of silence save the steady fall of rain, I heard Cong give an exuberant shout.

"We do not die!"

"There's still time. Follow me!" I pushed myself to my feet and turned, racing into a wall of choking black cannon smoke. Though gunpowder residue burned my eyes, I charged forth blindly and reloaded my pistol by feel along the way, knowing that Cong was struggling to keep me in view.

Transmitting into my radio while on the run, I shouted, "We're breaching! Get your men here now."

Zixin responded, "*Moving.*"

I had just keyed the mic to respond when I crashed into a wet human shape and fell, the figure above me laughing loudly—one of the augmenting fighters, having a great time ridiculing my panicked rush away from the bunker.

"Peng, hit the building!" I yelled from the ground.

The cannon's long barrel was already traversing toward the depot, a fourteen-foot horizontal column of steel choosing its next subject to obliterate. Once it stopped, I felt a chilling rush of fear that it would at that moment malfunction and we'd have to attempt a door breach without equipment.

But the cannon roared to life one last time. In his bloodlust, Peng had decided that the first few rounds weren't enough—why climb through a small hole when you can simply make the hole three times bigger? So he kept shooting, turning a considerable section of depot wall into a vaporous cloud of white that rose into the rain.

He stopped firing, and amid the echo of his final shot I yelled, "ADVANCE!"

Tiao was first into the breach, followed by Peng and two of the extra fighters. That put four assault rifles into our objective building before I crossed the threshold with my 9mm pistol, a weapon almost feloniously inadequate for room clearing.

I crossed through the hole into a rubble-filled room, clouds of white dust from incinerated cinderblock making the space appear as an impassable obstacle. I held my breath and plunged inside anyway, waving my free arm in front of me until I reached an interior wall, then felt along it until I found a doorway. The air started to clear as I entered a main storage room to discover a free-for-all in progress.

Tiao was on the floor, dead, his contorted body just inside the doorway next to a fallen enemy soldier. Peng was inexplicably on the back of another junta fighter, trying to choke him as one of our supporting Kokang fighters slammed his rifle stock into the enemy's chest in an attempt to take him down without injuring Peng. In the far corner, the remaining fighter who'd entered ahead of me was in a close-range shootout with another enemy taking cover behind a stack of wooden crates.

I raced through the main storage room and past the next doorway on my route toward the item.

An advancing enemy soldier almost ran into me as he charged toward the sound of fighting that followed anti-aircraft fire ripping through the building. Two chest shots from my pistol dropped him and exposed another soldier several yards behind him, stopping in place to raise his Type 95 too fast for me to take careful aim.

I shot him a half dozen times in the torso, then took off at a run and vaulted his body before it had time to settle. I needed a rifle but couldn't bring myself to expend valuable seconds getting one off the dead enemy— we were close to the item, and possibly even closer to an enemy counterattack that we wouldn't be able to hold off.

Another pair of soldiers appeared through the smoky darkness, and I opened fire while advancing rapidly toward them. The first fell and I directed my fire to the second, scoring two hits that slowed his reaction but left him standing. Then my pistol went empty—I vaguely registered the jolting click of the slide locking to the rear—and I let it fall from my grip as I slid the knife free from my kit.

The last man and I were both screaming as we converged on each other. Grabbing his rifle barrel with my free hand, I plunged the knife into his stomach as hard as I could.

I felt a visceral repugnance as my blade punctured his abdomen, the aversion heightened a moment later when I canted it upward and drove it behind his ribs into vital organs. Our shouts ended together, mine out of disgust and his trailing into a wheezing breath as a horrible septic odor blasted into the space. I yanked my knife free and pushed him to the side.

Armed with nothing but a blade, I crossed into the final room.

There, I saw Cetan.

My interrogator was crouched in the corner, by all appearances trying to avoid the battle and quite horrified that it had now come to him. He had no weapon, and his eyes displayed a desperate horror upon seeing me burst through the door with a blood-covered knife.

I took a sudden half-step toward him, and this was all it took for Cetan to submit into a fetal slump, palms open toward me in surrender. Turning away, I saw a metal filing cabinet wedged between a desk and a cluster of rusted steel drums—the location of the item, just as it had been described.

I fell to my knees before the cabinet, dropping the knife and pulling open the drawer with my left hand. Rows of brick-sized boxes lined the space within, each commercially packaged with Chinese script. Flinging them out of the drawer one at a time, I caught sight of the one box in the bunch marked with an innocuous red dot sticker in the corner.

I pulled it free and clutched it in my grasp, my right hand marring its surface with the hot, greasy blood of the soldier I'd stabbed. Distant battle sounds raged outside the building but I couldn't bring myself to react, staring instead at the box as my head swam in a cloud of almost opioid euphoria. At last I held the item, had achieved possession against all odds. It was a direct representation of Ian's freedom, of avenging all those I'd lost along the way, of the Handler's certain death.

Sudden gunshots in the room startled me, and I flung my head toward Cetan—a possible threat I'd unforgivably left alive in my rush to get to the item.

But Cetan's body was crumpling with the eruptions of blood that spread across his torso like boils, his shooter blasting away in an overkill of gunfire that didn't end until my interrogator had fallen forward into a prostration of death.

I looked to the doorway to see Cong shouting as he lowered his rifle from a firing position.

"—now! Mr. David, we must go, now!"

Gripping the box as if it would disappear into thin air if dropped, I shouted, "EXFIL, EXFIL, EXFIL!"

We consolidated with the survivors of our raiding party. Exiting the far side of the building into a downpour of rain that had become near-torrential, I heard the crackling pops of gunfire around us. My stab of fear subsided as I realized the sound was Zixin's perimeter defense element, now trading fire with Myanmar troops to cover our escape.

With the item in hand, our raiding party sprinted through sheets of rain, along our escape route, and back to freedom.

VICTORY

Omnis vir enim sui

-Every man for himself

13

Kun met me at the safe house door upon our return, the fall of darkness accelerated by the storm clouds that continued unleashing a monsoon of rain.

I handed him the box. "I'm sorry about Tiao. We could not recover his body without being killed by army reinforcements."

Kun accepted the box and turned it over in his hands, fondly stroking the sticker marking it from the rest of the batch.

"Tiao understood the risk. Please, come with me."

I followed him to his workshop, a room converted into a bizarre hybrid of tool shop and laboratory. He took a seat before a weathered bench, the wall above it covered in shelves hosting hardware, power tools, and medical supplies. He set the box down on his workbench and recovered a scalpel from a drawer, removing the plastic sheath to expose a paper-thin blade.

I surveyed the room, seeing everything from biohazard disposal boxes to equipment for forging blades. "You seem very willing to accept Tiao's loss."

He countered, "We play these odds willingly. These are the sacrifices we make."

"Yes," I agreed. "But not for money."

"You overestimate my virtue."

Using the scalpel to delicately slice the seals at the box seams, he lifted the lid. I peered inside to see a watch—gaudy, fake, the view of its dial warped by the cheap crystal.

"Kun," I sighed, wiping a slick of hair away from my face, "you may be deeply involved in everything illegal in this region, but you're no ruthless criminal—you still removed your shoes in the Buddhist temple when we met."

"So? This is our custom."

"You're a smart man. So are Peng and Cong. If this was about providing a decent living, you could do it any number of ways. You're interested in the type of profit that isn't available legally in this part of the world, and there are only two reasons for that."

Setting the watch aside, he removed the display panel from the box and laid it upside down on the desk. "There is only one. Greed."

"For most, yes. For people like you there's another."

"Oh?"

"Family."

He picked up the scalpel and froze. His face aged further before me, the creases in his skin deepening.

I asked, "Where are they?"

"Safe. In China."

Nodding slowly, I continued, "Provided the best education and opportunity, paid for by the sacrifices of a few members who cross the border to continue the family craft. Does your extended family in China know what you do to support them?"

"No. Never. They are establishing their own ventures within the law, and soon will require no more financing from me. But in the meantime they need money for the transition to legitimacy—it is quite a difficult leap to make."

I thought of Parvaneh. Her plan to inherit the throne and leverage a transnational crime syndicate to create opportunity for the impoverished masses was so ambitious that she either couldn't conceive of the challenges or understood them all too well and was willing to dedicate her life to their pursuit. Either way, she had noble intentions that her father, the Handler, was incapable of comprehending, much less implementing.

Brushing the thought aside, I continued, "That's got to be tough—they benefit from your sacrifices but don't know the pains you've undergone on their behalf."

Kun didn't skip a beat. "The soldier's dilemma, yes? Few care what their protectors undergo, and those who care can never understand. Except the pains we take for family are never as meaningless as governments sending their armies to slaughter."

"What's that supposed to mean?"

Lightly holding the scalpel, he used the tip to precisely separate the box display panel into two pieces at the seam.

Taped to the inside of one section was an inch-long glass vial.

He grinned at the sight of the vial, then frowned before he replied, "Is Iraq any better off for your nation's intervention? Is Afghanistan?"

I hesitated, swallowing before I managed, "I'm not a foreign policy expert."

"Nor do you have to be to answer my question. But we digress from our present agenda." He plucked the tape from the glass vial, lifting it for me to see without the slightest tremor in his elderly hand. A clear liquid was encapsulated inside—it could have been a few drops of water for all I knew.

I shrugged. "That's what all this has been for?"

"This, David, is beyond fentanyl."

"Fentanyl?"

He chuckled to himself as he set the vial in a glass bowl atop his workbench.

"A synthetic opioid painkiller that could serve your employer's purposes quite well. But it is known to be lethal, and advanced scanners will test for it. However"—he indicated the vial—"*this* is an acetyl fentanyl derivative, an extremely recent breakthrough at a single laboratory in China. They found a method to alter the fentanyl synthesis to produce a substance virtually undetectable by even the most modern chemical scanners. A small quantity was stolen from the lab and transported across the border while under chase from Chinese authorities."

The words elicited a rush of exhilaration within me. I'd wondered why Sage had sent me to Myanmar, and it all suddenly made perfect sense: the Handler either directly controlled or had detailed intelligence on nearly every facility capable of producing cutting-edge synthetic poisons. Sage needed something sufficiently exotic to make it through the Handler's security screening procedures, yet produced outside of the monitored assassination labs.

And in Southeast Asia, she'd found the intersection of both.

Kun watched me strangely now, waiting for me to process everything he just said. I swallowed hard. "In the cave, you said you needed to combine this with another item before I can return. What is it?"

"The other"—he reached into a workshop drawer to procure an object for me to observe—"is this."

In his hand was an immense fountain pen the size and shape of a cigar. I recognized it at once—it was the same pen with a swirling gold dragon that the Handler had used to sign the order that had sent me into a mole hunt against Sage.

Did Kun know who the target was? Sage had surely kept it a secret.

I tried to conceal my recognition of the writing instrument with the words, "So if the poison doesn't work, we can club the target to death with that pen?"

Kun didn't seem amused. "This is a fountain pen replica, recreating very demanding specifications. I am told the original was modeled in Japan by the old masters around the turn of the century. It would be of incalculable worth today. But alas, while records of its creation exist in archives, the actual pen has been missing for decades." Then he shot me a knowing look, one wizened gray eyebrow tilting with humor. "But I suspect that whoever possesses it will be dead very, very soon following your return to North America."

"So you're going to put the poison on the pen?"

"First I will infuse a thin sheet of transparent gel with the derivative. Then I must apply it to the grip section of the replica fountain pen—this keeps the lethal portion protected by the pen cap until the victim removes it and holds the pen to write. The amount of fingertip pressure to hold a pen of this weight will achieve instant transdermal absorption."

"Instant transdermal absorption?" I repeated, waving my hand over his workbench. "The scalpels, the medical supplies...you're a doctor, aren't you?"

Kun replied in a strange, almost wistful tone, "My previous career is not who I am now." He seemed embarrassed not that I had deduced this fact about his past but that I'd spoken it and thus forced him to relive the memory. "But we do not shed our experiences just because we have since crossed into crime. In that regard I suspect I am no more a doctor than you are a soldier. Men like you and me were not always criminals, no?"

"No, we weren't. And as a *former* soldier, I told you that I could retrieve this item with the help of your men. Now I need your assurance as a former doctor that this will work. When it is used, there will be extensive medical equipment and staff on hand. If the target survives for any reason—"

He dismissed my concern with a simple shake of his head, interjecting, "Due to the potency of the derivative and the concentration at which I shall infuse the gel, death will occur within seconds. Your target can be on life support at the time of contact, it will not help him or her."

I recalled the Handler in his office, using his pen to sign the order for my deep cover mission against Sage. Then I pictured him slumping dead on his desk before having time to seal the envelope with wax.

Smiling at the thought, I asked, "How is the target going to die?"

"Massive respiratory depression."

"So the target will simply...stop breathing?"

"Quite violently, I assure you. At the cellular level, there are receptors that relay oxygen and carbon dioxide levels to the brain, and the brain tells the lungs to breathe. By binding this substance with the receptors, it short-circuits the brain's ability to ascertain vital gas levels in the body, and therefore the very process by which it operates the lungs. This"—he reached into the glass bowl and plucked the vial out, lifting it between thumb and forefinger to emphasize his point—"is the chemical equivalent of an atomic bomb against the body. Complete and total destruction, absolutely irreversible."

I realized I'd slid closer to Kun in the course of his speech, hanging on his every word. Taking a step back, I managed, "I look forward to returning it to my employer."

"As you should. Any one of you could have died on that mission—but not anyone could have recovered the item. When you wanted to enter Laukkai by yourself, I was fearful for you—for good reason, as things came to pass. But how you led the others into the depot was brilliant. Eventually, I think, strategy will suit you better than soldiering. Prove me right by living until that day."

"I'll try not to let you down," I mumbled, feeling both flattered and strangely uneasy about his assessment.

He seemed to sense my discomfort, easily changing the subject. "You know, in three decades I have never failed a client on a commission. This time would have been particularly embarrassing"—he smiled good-naturedly—"because I fucking hate the junta."

"It was my pleasure to assist with your problem." I took a breath, deciding to test the waters. "But if we may speak outside the bounds of this particular order, I have a small personal request."

He swept one hand in a self-assured wave. "Consider your request granted, if within my power."

I nodded. "Zixin left Cong and me to die before Peng seized the cannon."

"So I heard."

"Then let me kill Zixin."

Kun looked away from me, bowing his head. "Eagles do not hunt flies, David. This is what you ask for?"

"Zixin earned it."

"I will grant you one favor only." He turned his face back to me, his cheeks colored with emotion, a determined set to his mouth at the prospect of allowing something he found objectionable. "And yes, you may choose to use it on Zixin."

"Why wouldn't I?"

"He left you and Cong for dead, but you did not die. Revenge is futile—you cannot change the past. You can, however, alter the course of future events. I advise that you consider your favor carefully in light of what I have just told you."

Everything in my history pounded against my brain, creating a pressure that I knew would be assuaged in a moment of murderous rage ending in Zixin's death. I had to forcibly restrain myself from demanding that in lieu of any alternatives, but by demanding, I'd be a slave to my past self.

Zixin, I thought, was a cowardly speck on the underside of my travels. His death would do nothing to assist Ian or me.

The Handler's death, by contrast, would.

How could I safeguard the prospect of his death when I already had the item in hand, and it was being configured into an assassination weapon of staggering lethality?

Bring back a spare.

I nodded my concession to Kun's advice, then said, "You'll have some poison compound remaining after finishing my employer's commission?"

"A very small amount."

"Make me a second pen."

He recoiled at the words. "This is not possible. The work that went into the replica took months—"

"Not a replica. Just an ordinary pen, treated in the same way."

"You asked for my assurance that the poison will work. As a former doctor, let me assure you that even if I treat a second pen with the remaining traces of gel, I cannot guarantee it will cause immediate death, or even death at all. I do not let anything leave my workshop unless I am certain it will perform as I intend."

"A policy that has crafted a well-deserved reputation over your decades of experience. A policy"—I placed a hand on his shoulder as I saw the objection grow in his eyes—"that I understand completely. This is a special request, not one tied to your reputation. There's a saying in my former army: two is one, one is none. Always bring a spare. You want me to ensure the future instead of avenging the past? A backup item is the way to do it."

His eyes closed in a prolonged blink as I saw his face relax. "Now you are growing instead of resorting to your past ways. You should do that more often, David: let the past exist as it was. Direct your energies forward, not back."

I gave him a nod of understanding, to which he concluded, "Once I apply the derivative, it will take several hours to bond with the pens. Get some rest, David. They will both be ready by morning, and then you shall travel home at last."

* * *

The next morning, I went to the rooftop to watch the sunrise. It was the first time I'd seen the neon orange blaze of sun permeating the horizon since I'd arrived in Myanmar five days earlier.

In that regard, Myanmar in monsoon season wasn't quite so different from the British Columbian wilderness: brief glimpses of sun between otherwise omnipresent dull gray cloud cover, a shapeless mist blanketing the sky. Weather's equivalent of depression, I mused, replicating the mind's perception in the atmosphere.

The fighting had stopped before midnight, and a hushed calm had since descended over Laukkai. To the west, densely packed rust-colored rooftops dotted rolling hills that extended to Myanmar's interior. In the other direction, a rolling morning mist crawled between the hunter green mountaintops across the border in China, a vision that induced the same feeling of serene tranquility as my previous wilderness exile. I looked to the craggy mountaintops splitting the brightening sky. For reasons I couldn't explain, the mountains soothed me—from the Smokies to Afghanistan, the Pacific Northwest to the Myanmar-China border, I sensed profound if momentary glimpses of inner peace alien to me in any other setting.

All I had to do now was bring the pen back to Sage, and my role in the Handler's death would be complete.

Yet I felt an inexplicable sense of dread, like some impending doom was lurking not for me but for something I cared about more desperately. I'd just secured the item and delivered it for final production, and was days away from freeing Ian at last. So why wasn't I ecstatic? Rather than satisfied, I felt almost plagued, cursed, the memory of my father's last moments replaying in my mind as I awaited my transport out of Myanmar. Some nagging thought lurked in the back of my mind, something I couldn't put my finger on.

"Mr. David," Cong said, "may I speak with you?"

I turned to see him standing hesitantly in the doorway to the roof, and gestured for him to have a seat.

"For you, Cong, I've got all the time in the world. What's on your mind?"

He sat beside me.

"Yesterday was my first battle."

"And what a battle it was." I glanced at him, thinking he looked much older than he had at the outset of our mission the day before. Combat had a way of aging its participants with undue haste. "Let me ask you a question: when it seemed like we were about to be overrun, did you feel scared or excited?"

"Scared."

"Good. Either is normal."

"What did you feel, Mr. David?" He spoke with intensity, like a failing student asking his professor one last question before the start of a final exam.

I considered the inquiry, wondering whether I should be honest or inspiring, and sided with honesty. "I felt nothing. And that means it's time to retire."

"So you are done? Forever?"

I scoffed. "Just getting warmed up, probably."

"How do you live with this? Or with Tiao dying like he did?"

"You've got the rest of your life to think about what could have gone differently on that mission, brother. That's the game in this business. Believe me."

"I could not sleep last night. Did you?"

"I don't sleep much anymore, Cong. Hell, if I'm not fighting or among people I've fought with, I feel like I'm a stranger to everyone and everything. I'm completely isolated, and everything's...surreal. Constantly numb, like everything I experience is absurdly superficial compared to combat. Does that make sense?"

He looked profoundly troubled, staring into the middle distance between our rooftop and the idyllic Asian landscape. "The man I shot...in the room, with the item. I keep seeing him. No gun. Trying to surrender...innocent."

"The man you shot in that room"—I focused on Cong intently—"was my interrogator. Take it from me, he was an evil man deserving of death. You didn't kill an innocent; you performed a necessary execution."

But his gaze was fixed, his mind lost. I put a hand on his arm. "Cong— listen to someone who's been doing this longer than a day."

He blinked his vision clear and whipped his head toward me, startled.

"You lost sleep last night, yeah." I gave a short sigh, feeling my chest begin to tighten with a fleeting emotion between anger and disgust. "But don't make that a lifelong occurrence. You're not me, and you've got plenty of gunfights left before you start losing your humanity. In the meantime, there's one thing you need to remember."

He nodded, receptive, looking for any straw to grasp. I could've told him anything in that moment and he would have held onto it, desperate.

"Anyone who joins a side during combat has entered the arena, and whatever happens, happens. Executions included. But there are true innocents in every fight, Cong. Too many of them. We're lucky here because most of the civilians have fled Laukkai, but that won't always be the case. One day you're going to do battle somewhere with a lot of people who want nothing to do with it.

"And when that day comes, you do your best to avoid killing innocent people. War involves collateral damage no matter what you do. But those who freely kill innocents will never get it off their soul. Once you break that, there's no coming back. Until you do," I concluded, "you're intact. Whole. You understand?"

Cong's features softened, a glimpse of youthfulness returning to his expression. "Yes. I think I do, Mr. David."

"Know what you do when it's all over, before you lose your soul?"

"No."

I thought of Boss's words to me at our final team dinner. "You put it all in that place inside that you don't speak of, the one that not even your wife will know about. Veterans have been doing that since the dawn of war, and one day it'll be your turn. Pack it up with all the horrible shit you've ever done and seen, and start over."

He nodded distantly and we lapsed into silence for a few moments, each observing the landscape in our own way. Suddenly a deep *thump* was followed by the whirring screech of a rocket ignition, and then a distant explosion initiated the rolling chatter of machineguns. Cong was startled by the sudden noise, but I didn't flinch. Fighting had begun for the day.

A voice behind us snapped, "Mr. David."

I turned to see Peng holding the door to the roof open with one arm, looking more solemn than I'd ever seen him.

"It is time," he said sharply. "Kun would like to speak with you."

* * *

I arrived downstairs to a flurry of men moving crates in and out of Kun's workshop, now a gutted shell being quickly packed up and loaded into a panel truck.

Kun slipped through the crowd, his face solemn.

"What's happening?" I asked.

"The war is over."

"Cong and I just heard the fighting resume—"

He put up a hand to interrupt. "You heard a battle, David. Not the war." Leaning in, he lowered his voice so the men moving his equipment couldn't hear. "Seven hundred Kokang fighters were just captured near the Nansan border gate with China. That is less than three kilometers east. The fighting will end before sunset, and I must be gone before the Myanmar troops have free rein in Laukkai."

"Where will you go? If the alliance with the Wa is broken, then…"

Kun shot me a stern glance, as if to say I should know better than to ask.

I concluded, "Forget everything I just said. I don't need to know."

"Your employer's commission has been completed," he announced. "Given the countermeasures this item was designed to bypass, and your insistence on a backup, you must be targeting someone special."

I nodded.

"President?" he asked. "Pope?"

I said nothing.

He shook his head. "No, you wouldn't have the budget you're paying. No, I think this will be used on the Handler."

My blood ran cold, a shudder racing up my spine to the base of my neck. But Kun chuckled merrily. "I look forward to hearing the news of your success. It brings me great joy to satisfy the needs of a client."

"Then I hope I'll have good news for you soon."

"After what you accomplished to recover the item, I trust that you will succeed."

I gave a shrug and admitted, "I'm not the assassin. Only the deliveryman."

"We shall see, David."

He looked at me curiously, as if he was about to expound on the thought. Instead he extended a hand in my direction, holding both the enormous fountain pen and an innocuous ballpoint in his closed fist.

I accepted them as he cleared his throat and said, "You will have one chance, and one chance only. Do not remove the cap of either pen, ever. The only person to remove the cap must be the target. Items like this only work with known quantities of poison, and with objects that only one person is known to touch. You have both in the replica fountain pen. But you have neither in your backup."

"If the first pen succeeds," I assured him, "then I'll destroy the second."

"See that you do. Now we must both go from this place forever."

I bowed my head to him. "Thank you for everything, Kun. Goodbye."

"Not goodbye, David." He clapped his hands on my shoulders, giving me a sudden brisk shake before releasing me. "I will see you later."

I felt my mouth sliding into an unconvinced grin. "Kun...I don't think you will."

"In this life? Perhaps not. But in the next?" He shrugged helplessly, a playful expression dancing across his face. "Who is to say?"

14

Four Days Later
September 2, 2009
Link-up Point, British Columbia

The air was clean and crisp as a powerful breeze swayed the tall pine forest all around me. After my stay in Asia, the wild, resinous smell was unmistakably North American, and it felt like home.

A combination of being passed from driver to driver and a five-mile off-road hike had led me to a curve in a winding dirt trail through the forest, barely wide enough for an ATV and marked by the vague imprints of tire passage. I checked my GPS again, seeing that I was in the right spot, plus or minus three meters—this was my link-up point, and now all I had to do was wait for Sage.

I heard an all-terrain vehicle approaching only a minute before I caught sight of it. Finally Sage's flat black ATV rolled into view, still laden with fuel cans and cargo bags. The driver wore a full-faced helmet with tinted visor down. Broad shoulders and no breasts: not Sage, but a man intending for his face to remain hidden.

A second ATV trailed behind, this one similarly equipped for long-range use but painted olive drab. A Caucasian man I'd never seen before drove it.

Both ATVs stopped beside me.

The lead driver shouted, his voice muffled within the helmet, "You have it?"

Squinting at his visor, I saw only a reflection of myself. "Yes. And I've got—"

"Give it to me. Now."

I handed him the fountain pen. He held it up to his visor, examining it closely.

"It's ready to go?"

"It's good."

"If there were any complications," he said gravely, "now's the time to tell me."

"There were none. Death within five seconds, guaranteed."

He wrapped it in a black cloth, then slipped it inside his jacket.

I reached for the backup ballpoint in my pocket. "I've also got—"

The man revved his ATV, carving a tight circle between the trees and back onto the trail before speeding off the way he'd come.

"Asshole," I muttered, replacing the ballpoint as the second ATV pulled up. This driver wore a pistol on his hip but was without a helmet, his sharp features and long blond hair tucked behind his ears.

"I'm Brett," he said. "Get on. I'm taking you back to the cabin."

"Where's Sage?"

"She's meeting us there."

Brett urgently gestured for me to get on the ATV behind him, and I hesitated. Something about Sage's absence struck me as unsettling, but what did it matter? Everything else was going according to plan. If this was some type of elaborate setup orchestrated by the Handler, then I was already caught. And it wouldn't have been the first time, either.

I got behind Brett on the ATV, and he accelerated forward down the trail.

It took us just over two hours to reach the cabin, and I spent the vast majority of that time in a state of relief bordering on ecstasy. This was the definition of the home stretch—Sage's scheme had gone undetected by the Handler or it never would have gotten this far. Given the pains I'd gone to in order to retrieve the item, there was no alternate reality in which Sage betrayed our agreement to free Ian while sending me to fight with the Outfit. I found myself smiling when the mountain terrain became increasingly more familiar as we approached the cabin. It seemed strangely fitting that I would finish this bizarre journey where it had begun, in the wilderness hideaway Sage had rigged for the effort.

But when we finally burst into the boulder-strewn clearing that hosted the cabin, I barely recognized it.

A twenty-foot-tall antenna stood upright in the field. It was held in place by a concentric arrangement of guy wires anchoring it to the ground, enabling radio communications from the depths of the forest. The cabin roof was now covered in solar panels.

My ATV driver Brett bounded up the stairs, pushing open the door and shouting, "Look alive, Dustin! The hero of Burma returns."

Brett slipped into the side room as I entered the cigarette smoke-filled cabin, finding it had been transformed into a command post. A table supported a mobile satellite phone and stacks of radios with hand mics attached to coiled cables, and the wooden walls were tacked with maps, radio brevity codes, and time sequences.

This wasn't an assassination; it was a full-blown coup.

The radio operator seated at the table looked up at me, his bearded jaw falling open, eyes squinting as he watched me. Like Brett, he had a pistol on his hip, and I didn't know if he wanted to fight or shake my hand as he stumbled out of his chair, thumping his knee against the table.

"You're David, aren't you?"

I took a half step back. "Yeah...we cool?"

"Of course! I mean—it's an honor to meet you. We can't believe you managed to get the item out of Myanmar once Laukkai fell—but you did. None of this would've been possible without you."

He shook my hand eagerly, his grip powerful but his voice high and nasally. The physical build of a commando with the mind of a radio nerd.

"Sure, man," I offered. "You're welcome, the service was my pleasure and other, you know, trite banalities." I glanced around the cabin, seeing that the blond ATV driver was kneeling in the side room arranging briefcases. One of them was open on the floor, lined from side to side with stacks of neatly bundled cash. Many such briefcases or bank account transfers had surely changed hands in the months leading up to this attempt. I was probably only looking at the remaining balance to be paid once everyone involved had delivered on their final commitment.

The two men in the cabin were a skeleton crew awaiting Sage's return, but I wondered how many more knew of the Handler's imminent death and were eagerly awaiting their final payment.

"So, how much longer?" I asked.

Dustin the radio operator stammered, "H-how much longer...until what?"

"Until he's fucking dead. The assassination, man. All of it."

"Of course!" He sat down and scooted his chair closer to the table, then began analyzing an open laptop. "The item has already made it into the Mist Palace, so it's getting placed in his office now. He's got a signing in thirty-two minutes, so he's dead within the hour. The next call we get from our man in place will be when it's done."

"Your man? You mean Sage?"

"Sage isn't placing it. She's on her way back here now."

"Then who's taking over for the Handler after his death?"

Dustin hesitated at this, retrieving a cigarette and snatching a butane lighter from the desk. "There'll be a...temporary incumbent. When we get the call that the Handler is dead, that individual will safeguard our return to the Mist Palace, and Sage will assume control upon arrival."

I caught the delay in his response and the delicate way with which he phrased the words "assume control." Whoever was taking command after the Handler's death didn't know he was going to be killed by Sage, that the real transition of power was a two-phase effort. She pulled the strings, her inside man risked it all to emplace the pen, and when she was done with him she'd simply kill him and assume the throne.

Given how she'd placed a knife to my throat, this detail didn't surprise me much. And it didn't matter. Ian would be a free man by sunset, and on his way home within days. I'd be on my way to South America, free of Parvaneh and the palace politics of the Organization. Why Jais had fought to be promoted there, I had no idea—the real action occurred at the Outfit.

I nodded to Dustin. "Good. What then?"

He fired up the cigarette between his lips, the thin hiss of the butane lighter shooting a blue-orange spike of flame. "She receives her in-briefs from the vicars, begins the transition—"

"What's this?" I asked, pointing to a map of Rio de Janeiro with a neatly compassed circle around a cluster of populated areas between the mountains and the sea: Rocinha. My slum battleground of a highly eventful trip to Brazil earlier that year.

"Ground zero," he answered, dropping the lighter and taking a drag. "The Handler's private nuke will be transported to Rio de Janeiro and placed in Rocinha for detonation within seventy-two hours of our regime change."

"Detonation? Why?" I blurted the words, patently unable to feign agreement with or even acceptance of what he was telling me. My chest was constricting with dread, breath quickening as I struggled to follow Dustin's response.

"Don't you see the genius? Rocinha is where the opposition group hunted the Handler's ambassador and heir. Sage is going to send a message: you hunted our people in your backyard, and we recovered them and retaliated."

"But the fallout...from a nuke in Rio—"

"It's contained by the mountains. Look, it's a small device, right? Blast radius contained to a ghetto sitting in the bowl of mountains between the wealthiest parts of Rio: Sao Conrado to the west, Leblon and Ipanema to the east, none of which will be harmed in the slightest. Sure, the tunnel under the mountains will be shut down for decontamination, but no real infrastructure will be harmed in the slightest."

I balked. "Except Rocinha."

"Well, yeah," he agreed. "Obviously that'll be mostly wiped from the map. Two hours after detonation we'll release a statement of responsibility by an Islamic extremist group. The civilized world will blame terrorists: there's a two-hundred-foot statue of Jesus in Rio, for Christ's sake. But the criminal underground will know, and the Organization's legitimacy will be secured for decades."

My mind began swimming with disbelief. The line between terrorism and what I had involuntarily become a part of—no, what I had singlehand-edly facilitated—was becoming increasingly more nebulous.

I assessed my situation. A holstered pistol on Dustin's hip, another handgun carried by the man who had driven me back to the cabin, and a mobile satellite phone on the desk. I checked about for other weapons and saw none.

"What's wrong?" Dustin asked. "You're awful quiet."

"Nothing." Minutes away from Sage's return, I thought, and less than an hour until the Handler was dead. "It's just that this is all a lot to take in. I spent months in this cabin, living on faith. And now..."

"Now the Handler's about to die."

"Yeah."

"Hard to believe, isn't it? Seemed like a long shot for all of us. But you're the one who went to Myanmar and pulled off the toughest part." He looked up at me admiringly, eyes squinting with pride as he concluded, "You made all this possible."

I turned toward the cabin door in a daze.

"Where are you going?" he called, lowering his cigarette in objection.

"I need some air." I waved a hand idly around my face. "Too much smoke in here."

"Sorry, man. But Sage will be back anytime now—don't be long."

"I won't."

I stumbled away from the lurking haze of cigarette smoke into the clean, fresh mountain air, the sun hitting my face through the treetops as a breeze washed over me.

At that moment I remembered the Rio pastor whose religious service I'd ended to use his chapel as an Alamo for my last stand. Shortly before he'd left me to a fatal confrontation with Agustin's kill team in the favela, the pastor had prayed a blessing over me, and in that moment one line was burned in my mind.

May you deliver him from sin and find him worthy to conquer a greater evil.

Now I was on the brink of everything I had been fighting for: Ian's free-dom, the Handler's death, and a one-way ticket to join the war in South America.

And in the process, I'd somehow enabled the total annihilation of

Rocinha. I'd personally delivered the highly enriched uranium back from Africa, unwittingly handing it over to people who would use it to build a bomb.

Now the substance I'd recovered from Somalia would incinerate thousands if not tens of thousands, all because of another item I'd just recovered in Myanmar.

My father's voice on his deathbed: *It's the only stain I'll never wash off my soul, son. Whatever you do in life, never harm the innocents. Swear it to me.*

I placed my hands on my knees, bent over double, and retched into the long grass.

RESURRECTION

Ordo ab chao

-Out of chaos comes order

15

"At this point we're just trying to keep him comfortable—"

"Doctor," the sheriff's deputy beside me interrupted. "This is Mr. Rivers's son, David. I got him here as fast as I could."

The doctor waved away the nurses and knelt to eye level with me, his chocolate hair precisely matching the shade of his eyes as he looked into mine.

"Your dad has been in a car accident, David. He's been badly hurt, and it's very important that you see him now."

"Stop stalling," I blurted, unable to think of anything else to say.

He looked at me strangely, then opened the door beside us to usher me in.

Two nurses were hunched over a hospital bed, their backs to us, until the doctor announced, "Let's give the patient a few moments with his son."

The nurses left, watching me with both sympathy and fear, and a moment later I saw him.

My father was lying on the bed, hooked up to machines that chirped and blinked, as I approached him.

His face was half-covered by bandages. The flesh of his visible cheek was singed red and mottled by blackened flesh. A single exposed eye wept profusely amid the burns, his pupil almost iridescent beneath a torrent of tears.

I didn't cry at first, instead feeling a strange detached sense of fascination and sorrow. "I'm sorry, Dad."

He replied in his Irish lilt, his tone as calm as I had ever heard it, "It's not your fault, son. Don't ever blame yourself—I've had this coming to me for some time now."

"What?"

"You're a smart boy, and if you ever look into it...I can't bear for you to hear from someone else. You deserve better from me."

My lower lip began to tremble, a void of desolate sadness opening within me for the first time. "Look into...what?"

The door opened and a priest entered, regally clutching a Bible to his side.

"Mr. Rivers," the priest began, "if you would like last rites we should—"

"Get your brainwashed, costumed arse out of here and take your fairy tale savior with you, you miserable bastard." His voice trailed into a ragged gasp as he finished, "I need to talk to my son."

The priest left, and my father lowered his voice so much that I had to lean in to hear him.

"It's a lie, boy."

I felt my eyes filling with hot tears as I managed, "What is?"

"All of it." He winced through an unseen wave of pain, blinking his eye quickly as he steeled his focus. "Everything I told you about my past and why I came to America is a lie. My name is a lie."

"Why wouldn't you just"—I sniffled hard, struggling not to cry—"tell me the truth?"

"In Ireland I worked with some of my countrymen to fight British rule. I did things, David. Horrible things. One of those things—the worst of the lot—ended up killing civilians. I didn't mean for it to, but it did. Families, David. Children killed, because of me."

Tears spilled over my eyelids and ran down my face, and I angrily wiped at them with the back of my hand as my father's tone grew harsher, more stern.

"It's the only stain I'll never wash off my soul, son. Whatever you do in life, never harm the innocents. Swear it to me."

I swallowed hard and nodded resolutely. "I promise."

"I fled to America not just from the British but also from the men I used to work with. Changed my name, met your mother. Tried to be a good man, to be a good father to you."

"You are," I croaked, a new torrent of scalding tears blurring the lower half of my vision. "You're my hero, Dad."

He reached for my hand and I gave it to him. His skin felt hot, leathery, as he squeezed my fingers. "It's never too late to become a better person, and the only failure in life is a failure to change for the better, every day and in whatever way one finds possible. Don't ever let a mistake define you. Look at what I meant to you, look at the man I raised, and you go do the same. Make your mark with the triumph of your spirit over the absurd and meaningless void we've been born into. And when you start to doubt yourself, I want you to know that—"

"To know what?"

His eye remained locked on mine, but it moved no more.

Everything sounded like I was underwater after that. White uniforms flooding the room, someone's hands pulling me back into the hall as if in slow motion. My view filled with whitewashed hospital walls amid the nauseating smell of antiseptic, and I never saw him again.

* * *

I threw up three times in quick succession, the contents of my stomach disappearing into the long grass outside the cabin.

Recovering from the effort, I stood and wiped my mouth with the back of my hand. Then I looked to the sky as if it held some answer, but I saw only treetops blotting out a light blue blanket overhead and so I started walking.

I wandered into the boulder-clustered field around the cabin, a space I'd explored tentatively for the first time over seven months ago. My head was churning in disgust as I recalled the swarming mass of civilians in the favela racing for their safety when the enemy shooters opened fire on the crowd, trying to kill me. Then the little girl who'd discovered me in her kitchen, the one I'd had to pull to safety as Agustin's kill team passed through. Her resentful expression after our parting encounter, the trauma on her psyche leaving my eyes stinging with tears as I walked out, unable to meet her gaze. I thought about the nuclear detonation amid the tightly packed homes, a fiery red mushroom cloud of carnage rising from the hillside slums between the jungled mountains of Rio.

Shaken, I walked slowly around the side of the cabin, then out back.

The ax was still wedged into the stump where I'd left it two weeks earlier, its handle canted forty-five degrees skyward beside my long-forgotten pile of chopped wood. I approached it with a dreamlike feeling of weightlessness.

I placed both palms on the handle, and its weathered surface fell easily into my grasp as I wrenched it free of the stump.

* * *

I edged the cabin door open with the toe of my boot.

Dustin the radio operator stubbed out his cigarette in an ashtray on the desk and looked up.

"You okay?" he asked.

My mouth suddenly felt parched. I couldn't speak. The pastor's voice in my mind: *I hope I see you again and feel the difference God's hand has worked in your life.*

Dustin watched me strangely. "What's the matter with you, bro? You look like you just saw a...ghost."

His voice faltered on the last word as his eyes fell upon the ax I held in one hand, close to my side, the heavy blade almost touching the cabin floor.

His gaze moved from the ax to my face as he squinted in disbelief. This wasn't happening—was it?

Then his chair scraped backward and he began to rise, reaching for the pistol on his hip.

"*BRETT!*"

The cabin roof was too low for an overhead swing. Instead I raised the blade at a sideways angle, almost hitting the wall beside me before I swung it into Dustin as hard as I could.

The ax struck him in the juncture between his shoulder and neck, cleaving his flesh and bone open. Blood erupted from the savage gash and he screamed horribly, the sheer force of my swing knocking his body into the table and scattering papers across the floor.

I yanked the ax free as I heard Brett's footsteps running from the adjacent room, and I managed to blindly swing the ax to my rear in a tight, carving blow. The heavy blade slammed into Brett's stomach as he entered. A great rattling howl of air exited his mouth as a hot splash of blood and entrails fell onto the floor. He followed his guts to the ground, sagging in place as I pulled the ax free.

He rolled onto his side, starting to draw the gun as his face turned an eerie shade of milky cream. I tried to pull the ax free as his pistol cleared the holster but it was still lodged in his belly. Releasing the ax handle, I raised a knee above my waist and stomped his head with my boot. I could feel the skin of his face sliding on muscle, skull fragments grinding together in a single explosion as his hand went limp and the pistol fell away, forgotten.

I turned to Dustin. He was splayed out on the floor, surrounded by the documents and maps of Sage's coup. He was still breathing, his eyes wide, though he was virtually paralyzed by my strike. His right hand rested on the floor beside the pistol on his belt, his fingers involuntarily quaking in the tremor of death. Blood pooled over the maps and papers that had scattered from my attack, the sheer volume making it inconceivable that he was still alive.

Yet he was.

I reached down and picked up Brett's abandoned pistol, then approached the radio operator until I stood beside his head. His wet eyes met mine, the expression one of terror, though his face was frozen in a stroke-like state.

A final line from the pastor's blessing ran through my mind, unsolicited.

If not here, then when all the great warriors of eternity are gathered around the fire of heaven.

Angling the barrel toward Dustin's head, I fired once and put him down like a rabid dog: a creature once innocent and loyal now corrupted by darkness so vile that the only redemption was death.

Sliding the pistol into my belt, I found the mobile satellite phone on the floor. It rested atop a single sheet of paper with the succession plan for the coup—a lone conspirator listed as the Handler's successor, taking control only to be killed by Sage when she returned.

As I read the name, everything became clear to me—how Sage had known about the Handler's test in advance, how she'd been able to fake my death.

I used Dustin's butane lighter to ignite the corner of the paper, then dropped the flaming page atop the cigarette butts in the ashtray and watched it burn to a blackened crisp. Then I looked around in a panic for a grid coordinate to my location. Sage was going to return soon, and I needed to ambush her with a pistol before she witnessed the bloodbath in her command post.

Unable to quickly find a grid location amid the debris, I snatched the satellite phone and ran outside.

* * *

Extending the phone's antenna and tilting it skyward, I hastily dialed the number I'd memorized before my feigned assassination attempt at the Executive *Karoga*—a direct line to the Handler.

The phone beeped an objection.

There was no satellite link.

I looked at the tree cover clustered overhead, frantically searching for a clear spot. Finding none, I raced to the side of the cabin and clambered up the hillside toward high ground.

I moved with a brisk sense of finality, following the route I'd taken many times before, my eyes riveted to the terrain features that guided my journey. Wandering off the trail and getting lost would be a devastating and possibly fatal blow to my plan—I was now fully committed, the evidence of my betrayal in plain view in the command post. This gave me considerable latitude with the Handler but meant nothing if I couldn't reach him before he touched the poisoned pen.

I finally emerged beside the crystalline hilltop lake I'd visited nearly every day of my isolation, approaching its bank where the sky was unobstructed. Through a break in the tree line on the far side, I saw the snow-covered slopes of faraway mountains.

I dialed the number once more, bringing the phone to my ear as I waited through a long series of beeps interspersed by silence. Holding the pistol in my right hand, I spun in a circle to make sure I was alone.

When the line connected, I heard the eerily monotone accent that sent a shudder down my spine.

The Handler said, "Am I speaking to a dead man?"

"Not anymore."

"Welcome back." He didn't sound surprised in the slightest. "What information do you have for me?"

"I don't have much time, so listen closely," I ordered, whirling around again to make sure no one had followed me uphill. "I know the plan to assassinate you. And it's too late for you to intervene."

"Why call if I cannot stop it?"

"You can't, but I still can. And don't try to cross me on this—I've got an insurance policy."

I was about to make a deal with the devil, but that deal—and the devil —were both things I desperately needed in that moment.

"What insurance?" he asked.

"You were obviously right to suspect Sage. But I've got the name of another inside conspirator that I won't divulge to you until you agree to my terms publicly—I want Parvaneh present to confirm, because your word means nothing to me."

"She will not be thrilled to see you, David, but if her assurance that I will honor the terms of our agreement—"

"Fuck the original agreement." I tensed my hand on the pistol. "Here are the new terms. Ian's no longer your slave. He will be freed from the Mist Palace, completely and for life. You'll still send me back to the Outfit to join the war in South America, but not as a shooter—I want to lead my own team. That's it. You've got three seconds to decide before I hang up and you die. I'm not sparing you to save Ian again."

One second of silence, then two.

"I accept," he declared. "Where are you?"

"I'll call you back when I can figure out my location. Then I need you to send the Outfit to get me—they're the only ones you can trust right now. Until then, lock down your compound. No one else in or out. Don't eat anything, don't touch anything, don't see anyone until I get there. Your conspirator is higher-ranking than you're going to—"

Two hands clenched on my right arm, flinging me sideways, followed by a knee strike to my elbow that caused the pistol to fall from my grip. I slammed into the wild grass surrounding the lake, releasing the satellite phone as I rolled to my side to defend myself.

A sharp kick to my face flung my head back, and I scrambled away on my hands to see Sage standing over me. Her hair was down, unkempt, eyes alight with fury as she knelt to pick up the satellite phone. Pressing a button to end the call, she flung it at me.

I raised an elbow as the phone struck me and fell to the ground.

"What did you SAY?" she screamed. Her face was alive with rage, veins in her throat bulging like worms crawling beneath her skin.

The fallen pistol was on the ground a few feet behind her, and I clambered to my feet.

"He knows." I wiped a slick of hot blood off my lip. "Your coup is over—"

As the last word left my mouth, she lunged forward and cracked a jab against my jaw, followed by a sharp uppercut into my gut that doubled me over.

"I saved your *life!*"

She grabbed my shoulders and drove her knee into my sternum, knocking the air from my lungs. I sagged into her grasp, unable to breathe.

"You'd be dead without *me!*"

She flung me to the ground, where I bounced and started to roll. Then she kicked me in the ribs with blinding speed.

"I would have given you *everything!*"

She swung another kick, which I managed to block as I grabbed her calf. Before I could twist her boot sideways to break her ankle, she slipped her foot free and drove a hard downward kick into my temple.

A deafening ring exploded in my skull, and I limply spat out a puddle of blood as I tried to suck in air, succeeding enough to clear my vision.

I rolled onto my back, the origami treetops over my head filtering sunlight and sky into bleary specks of light scattered across my blurred vision.

I gasped, "You were going to nuke Rocinha."

"A small payload!" she shouted back, indignant. "It would have been contained by the mountains, and the only people affected would be put out of their misery from the shithole slum they're imprisoned in!"

She let me struggle to my feet, clutching a rib throbbing painfully from her kick. Everything hurt now—head, chest, sides—and I vaguely took in the dark shape of the pistol in the grass several meters away.

"If I were you I'd start running," I said, staggering a few steps toward my gun. "They'll be here any second."

"They're not going to catch me, David. I will kill the Handler—but now I'm coming after Ian too. I'll spend a week carving him up, and I *will* detonate that device in Rocinha. You've merely delayed the inevitable—"

I lunged toward the gun.

She intercepted me effortlessly, delivering a flurry of blows faster than I could process where they impacted. Her strength was superhuman, her reflexes beyond lightning fast. Our fight in the cabin had been a crude performance on her part, designed to let me perceive I had a fighting chance.

Now she was delivering jabs, hooks, kicks for no reason other than to punish me. Devoid of a firearm, I wasn't a worthy opponent; her coup had been forever derailed, and after killing me on the hilltop, she'd be on the run for what would likely be an extremely short existence.

But first, she was going to impart her rage upon me.

Her melee stopped as she screamed, "You want that gun? Go for it!"

I flung myself toward the pistol, landing with my arm outstretched. My fingertips scraped across it for the briefest of moments; I felt its cool surface but she dragged me backwards before I could grasp it.

I swung an elbow back at her, but she parried my blow and forced the side of my face to the soft ground.

The earthy smell of pine and soil filled my nostrils as I spoke into the matted grass.

"I'd rather die than help you kill innocent people."

She flipped me onto my back, both hands on my throat, crushing the air and blood away from my brain.

"Oh, David." She leaned in and whispered, "There's more to serving humanity than saving lives."

As she squeezed her hands harder around my esophagus, the dizzying pain in my head compounded exponentially. I lacked the coherence to swing a blow, remove her hands, or do anything but lie there and let the life pass from me.

With the last of my strength, I reached into my pocket and slipped trembling fingertips around the ballpoint pen. Pulling it out, I thumbed the cap off to expose the grip and raised it toward Sage's muscled forearm.

But I was losing consciousness too fast, my vision receding to a pinpoint of focus, and my hand fell to the grass, almost losing the pen. Then I thought of the girl in the favela, and with the final whisper of life within me, I blindly drove the pen toward her hands on my throat.

The pen stopped against flesh, though whether hers or mine I couldn't tell. The pain in my trachea was too immense to distinguish where my throat ended and her choking hands began.

With every waning vestige of focus I had left, I pressed the pen.

Sage's high-pitched scream echoed in the forest. The pressure on my jugular vanished as her weight on my body lifted, though I could neither breathe nor see. I choked hollowly for air, unable to recover.

A single dot of light appeared in my vision, growing wider until blurry forms transformed into treetops, then a weak gasp of breath filled my lungs shallowly, followed by another as I drew in air with the desperation of a dying man.

As my sight returned I heard a horrible, wraithlike cry all around me. I lifted my head to see Sage on the ground a few meters away, crawling on her side and clutching one hand by the wrist.

"...BURNS! IT BURNS! IT BURN—"

I dropped the pen, flipped to my stomach, and pulled myself forward along the ground with one hand, sweeping the other across the grass until I felt the polymer grip of the Glock. Clutching it like it was the sole life raft in an endless stormy ocean, I rolled onto my back. I spread my legs, holding the pistol over my crotch in a two-handed grip as I aimed at Sage.

Despite my best attempts to steady the gun, the white orb of its front sight post waved in wide, lazy circles around Sage's once beautiful face. She was silent now, her features frozen in a horrid death shroud, mouth agape like a grinning skull.

I pulled the trigger.

The tousled red hair at the corner of her scalp fluttered as a chunk of the skull beneath it blew outward, spilling a puff of brain matter. She didn't move.

I tried to steady the sights, firing again.

A neat, circular glimmer of light flickered through her open mouth as sunlight appeared through the hole now bored at the back of her throat. My third shot struck her through the right eye, a pile of salmon-colored flesh falling forward but her head remaining immobile.

I struggled to my knees, leaning back on my heels to gain as much stability as I could in my weakened state. Even in death I feared her, what she had become, what she had been all along unbeknownst to me. Even in her death, I was horrified by what she was going to do to Rocinha.

Leveling the pistol at her, I fired over and over until the slide locked back to the rear and there was nothing left of her face to shoot.

16

The Outfit team that recovered me first cleared the cabin, then detained me and moved uphill to recover Sage's body at my direction. Behind them came a cleanup crew—men and women who scoured the cabin with evidence bags, inventorying the contents and filing them for analysis by the Intelligence Directorate. A biohazard team moved in with black lights and industrial cleaning equipment—by the time they were done, not a trace of forensic evidence would remain. The cabin would be left to lapse back into a dusty state of disrepair.

My last glance of the cabin revealed a single man in a biohazard suit entering the doorway with a folded body bag in each hand. Then the scene was gone in a flash, replaced by the forest as an ATV whisked me off down the trail and back to the Mist Palace.

***

I returned to the Mist Palace as a prisoner.

I wore handcuffs, leg irons, and blacked-out goggles as I was led through a building to places unknown. The men transporting me had been forceful but not overly so, and I didn't resist them—after all, the thwarted coup attempt was less than two hours old and I'd told the Handler to lock down everything until I could speak to him personally. He entrusted his security to professionals, and they weren't about to let me waltz through on reputation alone. Hell, I'd been a part of the assassination plot until I decided that Sage was worse than the Handler, so I wasn't entitled to any special treatment. That much was fine by me—as long as Ian was freed.

I was finally seated and my goggles removed.

The first person I saw was Ishway.

He stood imperially to my left, dwarfing a podium holding his leather-bound ledger. Ishway was attired as I'd always seen him—suit and dress shirt, pocket square and tie, each of different patterns that nonetheless combined to some unified whole of fashionable splendor. His black hair was pulled into a low bun as usual, but this time his severe eyebrows seemed relaxed, as though he was confident about the game that was about to ensue.

"Welcome back, Mr. Rivers."

My chair was situated at the center of a scarlet carpet extending to a long wooden panel that rose to chest height of the three figures seated behind it—the three chief vicars I'd met at the Executive *Karoga*. Omari, the portly, mustached chef; Watts, the silver-haired movie star with streaks of facial scarring; and Yosef, the dwarf in a black yarmulke, all looking fairly tense about the current situation. Only two bodyguards were present, both holding slung submachine guns. It seemed abnormally light security; no doubt the Handler was limiting witnesses to whatever proceedings were about to occur.

"Where's the Handler?" I asked, shifting to observe my surroundings as the chains between my wrists and ankles clanked.

Ishway replied, "The One will join us momentarily, upon which time we will begin our open assembly."

An elevated seating area held several empty chairs, with one desk raised above the rest—the Handler's throne, waiting for its sole occupant.

I glanced irritably at the vicars, all watching me.

"And an open assembly is...what, exactly?"

At first glance, we could have been in a chapel of sorts. But as the positioning of the seats and the status of those present began to sink in, I realized the truth was something far worse.

I was in a courtroom.

Ishway shifted behind the podium. "The high leadership will advise the One about your circumstances, and after hearing all their counsel he shall determine his final ruling."

"What do you mean, his final ruling? The Handler already gave me his word of honor. Is that worth nothing here?"

Watts's Boston drawl was delivered with a tilt of his silver head. "Preliminary word, yes. But no agreement is sacred if it is detrimental to the Organization. That determination is made in an open assembly. The Organization"—he grinned slightly—"comes first in all things."

I laughed incredulously, looking from the vicars to Ishway and back again. My gaze settled on the nearest bodyguard, objectively watching me with his submachine gun in hand.

Shaking my head, I replied, "Be that as it may, I alone know the identity of the remaining conspirator—to say nothing of the means of assassination, which is, I regret to inform you, still very much in play."

Omari spoke up at this, his stern tone contrasting with the jovial nature I'd encountered as he cooked for the *karoga*. "We have other means of extracting that information from you, Mr. Rivers. Do you doubt this?"

Shit. "No, that ah...that pretty much all checks out."

What had I expected? The Handler had told me whatever it took to bring me back, but honor meant nothing to him unless it could be neatly situated amid the strategic landscape he'd crafted around himself. If I couldn't define some overarching importance to my stated terms after furthering Sage's scheme, I was dead, and so was Ian.

Around the world and back again, only to be stuck at square one—a prisoner who'd escaped and now slipped back into his cell in the hopes of escaping again, and Ian no more free than he was at the outset of my journey.

A door opened and a new procession filed in: the Handler, followed by his personal bodyguard, Racegun. Then Parvaneh, followed by her personal bodyguard, Micah.

The Handler and Parvaneh took seats in the open chairs, with Racegun and Micah standing beside their respective charges.

Parvaneh enraptured me. She was stunning—tall and lean, her electric green eyes floating across the room without looking at me. Her shining dark hair, much longer than I had last seen it, descended across her neck and down one shoulder.

The sight of her disarmed me completely—I'd entered that room feeling brash, bold, vindicated in finally having some negotiating power with the Handler. Finding that I still had to plead my case despite stopping Sage's plot was like a sucker punch to the gut. But the sight of Parvaneh took the life out of me.

After everything I'd done to her, manipulating her affections to get closer to assassinating her father, I wanted to collapse at her feet and beg for forgiveness.

She didn't meet my gaze, instead staring resolutely ahead. Micah, by contrast, watched me with the same contempt he always had.

Ishway announced, "This open assembly begins with a statement by the One. Sir, the floor is yours."

The Handler leaned forward from his vantage point at the highest desk in the room. With his slanted Roman nose jutting out from his gaunt face, he looked like a vulture scanning the desert as he addressed his court.

"This January, David attempted to kill me at the Executive *Karoga*. He was detained and transferred to Sage for interrogation and summary execution. Those of you here today knew as much, but there is one detail kept secret by design. This entire sequence of events was carefully scripted, and David was sent into play as a deep-cover agent to confirm or deny Sage's loyalty to this Organization.

"Sage took David for execution. But she must have held advance knowledge of my plan, for the biometric confirmation of the corpse's remains was clearly mistaken. And so, on January 31 of this year, David was declared dead, Sage's loyalty was earnestly confirmed, and Avner Ian Greenberg joined the ranks of the Intelligence Directorate.

"Thus imagine my surprise this morning when I received a call from a dead man: David Rivers, demanding a new arrangement to stop an assassination attempt that had progressed too far for me to stop it. In exchange for his terms being agreed to, David has assured me that he will unveil the identity of a remaining conspirator among our ranks."

I felt a pang of relief at the Handler publicly admitting our deal—

maybe he would hold up his end after all. The assemblage looked considerably less relieved, seeming pensive about the proceedings. Bizarrely, the guilty party appeared the most composed short of the Handler himself. No fear of being exposed, or else knowing it was too late to stop it.

"The Outfit team sent to recover David also discovered Sage's body, along with two others. The latter two were killed with an ax. So here we are, not to determine the exact details of David's absence—that much will be made startlingly clear during an extended debrief in the coming days—nor to uncover the remaining traitor in our midst. That traitor"—a crooked grin spread across the Handler's face—"will be found regardless.

"Instead we are here to inform my ruling on David Clayton Rivers and his two requested terms: that he rejoin the Outfit as a team leader in the ongoing war, and that Avner Ian Greenberg be released from his service to the Organization. Let us begin."

The Handler leaned back in his chair, cutting his eyes to the vicars as Ishway spoke.

"The assembly will begin with the counsel of the Chief Vicar of Finance. Vicar Omari, speak the truth."

Omari pushed back his chair and stood, thoughtfully stroking his mustache for a pregnant pause. Then his Kenyan accent filled the room.

"Now that the One's plan is revealed after being brilliantly withheld from us until now, I can be certain of only one thing."

Omari's eyes turned to mine, his expression so far removed from the chef I'd met in January that I barely recognized him.

"David is not to be trusted. By admission of facts, he was an assassin before being conscripted by the One. When Sage's opportunity arose, David veritably leapt at the chance to become an assassin once again. His return to us occurred only when it suited his whims.

"This Organization was not built upon extending benevolence to traitors, particularly those who very nearly assassinate its leader. My judgment is that the remaining conspirator be revealed through the ample means available to us, and once known, that David meets the same fate. Traitors earn traitors' justice, and that justice does not carry with it the nuances of mitigating circumstances. I have withheld nothing from the assembly."

Omari had barely finished seating himself before Ishway spoke again.

"The assembly will now hear the counsel of the Chief Vicar of Intelligence. Vicar Yosef, speak the truth."

The short man in the yarmulke stood, black eyes darting furtively behind his glasses. I tilted my head to him, having never heard him speak.

When he did, it was with a quick, raspy beat, his accent Israeli.

"My counsel begins not with David but with his friend Ian." He looked at the Handler and flashed an eerily predatory smile. "Ian proved most useful in targeting the South American network. I soon transferred him to the cell responsible for locating high-value individuals, including the highest leader, Ribeiro. I do not support the release of Ian, for his contributions to the Intelligence Directorate are just beginning.

"As for David Rivers, he has proven that subversion, manipulation, and acts of incredible violence are as natural to him as breathing. Rather than let these virtues atrophy at the Outfit, assign him to the Intelligence Directorate, where I have a variety of assignments more suited to his singularities.

"Finally, David and Ian are not two but one. When employed with the knowledge that the other's life depends on their effectiveness in a given capacity, both are invaluable. Let us engage both accordingly, not release one and send the other to toil in common labor. Your Grace, I have withheld nothing from the assembly."

Yosef took his seat with a satisfied expression. For his diminutive size, this man was a monster among monsters—and in the company of the Handler, that title was no small feat.

Ishway boomed, "The Chief Vicar of Defense will provide his counsel. Vicar Watts, speak the truth."

Watts brushed a lock of silver hair from his brow, slid his chair backward, and pushed himself up by the armrests to a standing posture as casually as if he were at a backyard barbeque.

"I'll keep this short and sweet. As far as David being a previous threat to the Organization, I believe that's mitigated by keeping him very far from the Mist Palace and, more importantly, from the One himself. Other than that? David has proven that he's damn fine with a gun, excels under pressure, and is able to hold his own in combat. I fully support a return to the Outfit."

I cracked a slight smile at Watts. He didn't return the expression.

"Now as for my thoughts on this kid commanding a team in South America? Not a chance. David hasn't got the experience, and frankly, he's not built for that kind of responsibility. I've read his psychological evaluation, and he's not even in control of his own mind. You put him in charge of Outfit shooters, he's going to get our people killed. I have withheld nothing from the assembly, sir."

My jaw dropped. The one glimmer of hope in my favor had shone and faded in the same breath, and the proceedings continued marching toward their inevitably disastrous conclusion.

"The chief vicars have spoken," Ishway announced. "Sir, would you like to call upon the counsel of anyone among the assembly before reaching a decision?"

"I would," the Handler replied.

"Yes, sir. Please state who you wish to—"

"Let us continue with you, Ishway. What is your judgment on the man before us?"

Ishway froze for a moment, visibly taken aback. He was used to being an aide, a personal assistant, absorbing the tasks that no one else wanted to do. Why was the Handler asking for his opinion?

"Very well, sir. I would contend, as I always have, that we are all making the best decisions we can with the information we have available. We are all products of our upbringing, our circumstances, our desires and demons both." He glanced to me with a blink of consideration, then continued, "David is no exception, and be what may of his decisions and his...methods, however unorthodox and however beneficial or detrimental to this Organization at times, one fact cannot be denied.

"He has proven that he will either serve the One or the One's enemies to save a friend. I suspect"—he eyed me for another long second before resuming—"that the threat to others' lives played a pivotal role in his decision to stop the conspiracy and return to us today. So I will offer no verdict on what to do with him now, only ask that those qualified to decide do so with the full awareness of what lies at the core of David's character. I have withheld nothing from the assembly."

The Handler leaned over his desk and said, "Micah."

Parvaneh's personal bodyguard stiffened. His auburn hair seemed to have thinned considerably since our return from Rio de Janeiro.

"Sir?"

"You have firsthand experience with David's conduct in Brazil. I will now hear your counsel on what becomes of him."

Micah cleared his throat once and swallowed, pausing to consider his words. "During our plight in Rio, David's responsiveness and tactical decision-making were of high caliber. He proved that he was willing to accept great risks on behalf of Parvaneh, risks that ranged from singlehandedly going against multiple enemy fighters all the way to taking three bullets to prevent her from getting shot.

"But I'd caution you, sir, that these decisions were not made out of calculated risk-taking. They were made out of a reckless disregard for his own life. From my observations, David's character is rooted solely in self-destructive tendencies.

"Finally, I agree with Vicar Watts on the matter of David's psyche. He's been formally diagnosed with depression, suicidal ideation, posttraumatic stress, and alcoholism. None of these have been treated formally or, to our knowledge, even informally. If he's going to be employed at the Outfit, it should be in a highly supervised capacity, not in a position of leadership that he's neither earned nor demonstrated any aptitude for. That is my opinion in full, sir, and I have withheld nothing from the assembly."

"Parvaneh," the Handler said abruptly. "David has been touted as your savior—have you anything to say for or against him?"

A stab of shame speared through my chest. For all the pain of listening to these men discuss my every fault with the full knowledge that my life and Ian's were trending toward disaster, it couldn't compare to the dread of Parvaneh's judgment.

Unable to face her, I looked down only to see the horror of my right boot. It was soaked in the blood of a man whose life I had extinguished by stomping on his skull, the remains of which were now drying a brown shade of crimson on the suede.

I forced my gaze back up to Parvaneh. She didn't stand, instead looked strangely conflicted from her seat. Strong, thick eyebrows and smoky eyes were marked by bright green irises, and her lips twisted with carefully concealed emotion.

Finally Parvaneh replied, "David has saved my life. Were it not for his intervention in Rio de Janeiro, my daughter Langley would be an orphan. I will never deny this, now or in the future."

I felt a rush of elation, tempered by the reality that she still wouldn't look at me. Her voice was flat but determined as she continued, "But David Rivers has also served on a team that brutally executed the father of my daughter. He has lied to infiltrate our Organization, and he tried to kill our leader."

I opened my mouth to call her name but stopped myself before the word could leave it.

"As for what becomes of him now, I must recuse myself from judgment. My decision would be made out of personal emotion, not professional necessity. I have withheld nothing."

She directed her eyes downward, saying nothing else.

The Handler nodded to Ishway, and Ishway looked to me.

"This assembly draws to a close. We will now hear from the accused. David Rivers, speak the truth."

I took a shuddering breath, then pushed myself to my feet with a jingle of chains against my handcuffs and leg irons. I looked over the faces present—Ishway unmoved, the Handler curious, Parvaneh blank, the three vicars unapologetic after unanimously condemning me, each in their own way, and finally Racegun and Micah vigilantly guarding the leader and heir of the Organization.

"Every time I set out to assassinate the Handler," I began, "I end up saving his life instead. You people should hire me to kill him more often."

Pausing, I observed everyone except Parvaneh watching me tensely.

"You've heard many things about me. That I'm a liar, a killer, a suicidal alcoholic. That I lied to infiltrate your ranks so I could kill the Handler. And these things are all true. But know this: my every action since crossing paths with your Organization last year was done not out of a desire for power but for vengeance. The Handler has killed everyone I cared about except one person, who has since been enslaved. What would you become capable of to stop someone who inflicted that kind of destruction on your world?

"Now you're wondering what brought me back here under those circumstances, so here it is. I just discovered that Sage was going to slaughter countless civilians in Rocinha, the slum in Rio where Parvaneh was very nearly killed. That loss of innocent people isn't worth my friend's freedom or his life, least of all mine.

"So you're right, Vicar Omari: I didn't stop her plot out of a compelling loyalty to the man who's taken everything from me. I did it to stop a greater evil. But my motivations shouldn't determine whether my terms are honored—only my results. And the Handler is alive, and the conspiracy against him dismantled.

"Vicar Watts and Micah have both expressed well-justified concerns about my leadership capacity in the Outfit. On this point, let it be known that I spent over six months sober in the wilderness before prevailing against great odds in Myanmar while leading men in combat. So while I can't negate the findings of my psychological tests for the Outfit last year, I *can* tell you that I am a different man than the one who entered Sage's control.

"I admit that I've done everything I stand accused of. Now you understand why. And there's only one person in this room that I owe an apology to."

I looked to Parvaneh, her eyes averted, her face marred with a suppressed agony that I alone had inflicted.

"Parvaneh—I'm sorry. I'm so very sorry for the pain I've caused you."

Then I swung my gaze to Yosef, the glint of light on his glasses blocking his eyes from my view.

"To Vicar Yosef, my career as a deep-cover agent is over. As I told the Handler when negotiating my return, I am no longer a puppet performing to save Ian. His freedom was earned when I ended Sage's conspiracy. This much was guaranteed to me by the Handler. For all our faults and allegiances, or as Ishway put it, 'our desires and demons both,' we are first and foremost men and women of our word, devoted to a personal code of ethics that serves us in the professions we've chosen."

I looked to the Handler, seeing only complete composure in his face, no concern and not a hint of surprise.

"We've had our issues, you and I. But here in this room and before Parvaneh, I've put aside our differences and spoken the truth. Now I look forward to seeing that you have done the same."

I lowered myself into my chair.

"Sir," Ishway asked the Handler, "would you like time to—"

"Silence," the Handler commanded. "I have reached my final decision on the matter of David Rivers."

I couldn't breathe as I waited for him to speak again, his golden eyes watched by everyone in the room.

With a slight tremor of his shoulders, the Handler issued his orders.

"Avner Ian Greenberg is hereby released from servitude to this Organization. He will depart today and, since I cannot permit a resurrection of the conspiracy between him and David, will remain under passive surveillance for the remainder of his life."

I blurted, "I want to see Ian before he leaves. Even an hour—"

"Your request is granted. Five minutes, supervised to ensure no breaches of operational security occur, and that will be the last time you ever see him. Now on to the second matter at hand. I hereby grant David Clayton Rivers command of an Outfit team, effective upon his arrival in South America within one week's time. His performance with this team will determine whether he is suited for higher levels of command in the future. This ruling becomes final upon David's compliance with revealing the remaining conspirator."

Watts looked mildly alarmed that his counsel was ignored, but said nothing.

The Handler looked to me with a stern nod. "David, you have heard my rulings before an open assembly. I command that you reveal the remaining conspirator now."

I didn't break eye contact, my stare locked onto the Handler's amber irises.

"Parvaneh, will your father honor these terms if I speak?"

His eyes began to blaze with fury.

"David, I caution you that I may just as easily alter my rulings until you have upheld your end—"

"Parvaneh," I called, louder this time, staring at the Handler in a battle of wills. "Will your father honor these terms?"

"David!" the Handler shouted, his face flushed, "reveal my enemy now or you and Ian will join him *IN DEATH!*"

Parvaneh's eyes shot my way, her green irises blurred with tears as she gave a slight nod.

"Yes," she half-whispered, then looked away.

I breathed a sigh of exhaustion both physical and emotional, then turned my head to the conspirator.

"Ishway," I said, "Sage was going to kill you afterward. Her plan was to become the Handler herself, not to serve under you. She just couldn't place the instrument of death without your help."

Ishway didn't flinch, didn't sag—instead he stood as regally as ever, watching me with an air of nonchalance as the Handler spoke to him.

"Do you deny this?"

Ishway swallowed and said, "This journey could end only one of two ways. I understood both alternatives well, and chose to forge onward. My only regret in life would have been not attempting to assume the position I know I am capable of. More so than you, sir." Then he addressed Parvaneh. "Long may you reign, and return this Organization to the glory it once had."

With that Ishway angled himself away from the nearest guard, then placed his hands behind his back.

"Interrogate him," the Handler commanded as a guard stepped forward to handcuff Ishway. "Quickly. Find the instrument of assassination—"

"The instrument is your pen," I said. "The fountain pen you've been using to sign operations into existence, including my mole hunt against Sage. I don't know where it is now, but the one sitting on your desk is an identical replica."

"Poison," he said simply.

I nodded. "The grip section beneath the cap has been coated in an advanced fentanyl derivative recently created at a laboratory in China and smuggled into Myanmar for application. It's currently undetectable to your most advanced sensors. Skin contact results in death, which, if Sage's demise is any indication, takes three to five seconds' worth of horrific screaming."

The guard swept out of the room with Ishway captive.

The Handler casually leaned back. "This assembly is closed. David, let us continue this conversation in a private venue."

* * *

I was led into the Handler's office without handcuffs, shackles, or blacked-out goggles—unspeakable privileges given the Organization's security protocol, but I didn't care. I only wanted to see Ian, and he wasn't present. The visitor's chair in the office was now empty, its leather cuffs hanging open as if in deference to the Handler's wide, ornate desk facing it. The desk was adorned with computer monitors that the Handler undoubtedly used to spin his web across oceans, trapping prey and expanding his reach.

There was something else now too, behind the desk—a tall cabinet, its walnut surfaces lavishly carved with the spiraling shapes of oriental dragons. It was a masterpiece, and one that I was seeing for the first time.

I stopped abruptly, Racegun's eyes locked on me as I pointed to the cabinet.

"That wasn't here before."

The Handler breezed past me. "Would you like to see what is in it?"

"You promised me I'd get to see Ian before he's freed. Stop stalling."

"See him you shall. But first we have one—no, actually two—matters to attend to. Come. Please."

I followed him to the cabinet, and he elegantly pulled the handles apart to reveal a lining of deep purple silk. The smell of richly oiled wood and leather billowed out as the interior was slowly illuminated by the gradually brightening display lights within.

I felt my stomach twist with strange pulls of emotion that had been dormant since childhood—the awakening of faculties I didn't know I had upon seeing my first pornography at age eight, the unrealized dimension of consciousness that unfolded within me the first time I got drunk four years later. Emotions I didn't know I had, perceptions I hadn't been able to conceive of until I'd felt them.

Like then, the sensation bubbling in me was a strange mix of shame and exhilaration and enlightenment, a cocktail too powerful and unnerving and unsettling for me to ever become remotely comfortable with, and yet there it was all the same.

And I couldn't take my eyes away from the object inside the cabinet.

The Handler didn't speak. He was respectful, allowing the moment to be, allowing me to form my own relationship with what I now stared at.

"My God," I stammered. "That's it, isn't it?"

"You brought the heart back from Somalia, David. And now, she lives."

I tried to speak, but all the air seemed to have been sucked out of the room. And I was floating, alive.

I could sense him smiling. "She was going to use this."

"On Rocinha," I managed. "As a demonstration of...oh, God. Look at it."

He stroked the top gently, his fingers dancing along its surface. Then he took my hand and placed it on the device in the cabinet. In that moment, no ancient artifact or alien life form could have commanded my attention to the same degree.

I felt his hand atop mine, and mine atop the object, my entire body tingling as if energized by a current that the device was emitting.

The Handler spoke quietly. "This is what power looks like, David. This *is* power." He removed his hand from mine, took a step back, and raised his voice to an authoritative tone. "And projecting it upon innocent civilians is a macabre performance reserved for those who mistake mayhem for righteousness."

"For once," I said, "you and I are in agreement."

"I sincerely believe that the more you see the way things work from my viewpoint, the more you will understand my rationale."

I took my hand away from it, breaking my stare and directing it to the Handler.

"Don't get carried away and think we're going to take warm showers together. You still created a nuclear device. And you almost lost goddamn control of it—that's not a wise execution of responsibility over this power you speak of."

"To the contrary, being in personal possession of such a monument is the ultimate responsibility."

"Not if you lose control of the device...or yourself."

"Control is my specialty, David."

I ignored his comment and glanced at the red pipes lining the ceiling, the self-constructed incineration system Sage had told me about. An eight-digit code known only to the Handler and his personal bodyguard would destroy the Organization at its core—a tantalizing possibility. I wanted to ask him what would happen if the nuke was set ablaze in the process but decided not to tip my hand.

Instead I asked, "Then what do you plan on using a nuclear device for?"

He responded coolly, "The usefulness of such a device is in the threat, not in its employment."

"You'd better be right."

Racegun said into his cuff, "Copy." Then he announced, "Everything's ready when you are, sir."

"Wonderful." The Handler beamed. "David, please follow me."

* * *

We walked down the corridor outside his office and through a heavy metal door leading to a familiar sight: a short hallway with three doors on the wall to our left. The middle one was open, and the Handler swept into it.

I knew what I'd see before we entered.

The room was built like a giant shower, with tiled walls and a floor beset by a large circular drain. The primary fixture was a throne of sorts—the electric chair in which I'd seen the Indian die, and had subsequently been placed in myself.

It was occupied, of course, by Ishway.

Gone was the sleek black hair swept into a high bun. They'd shaved his head just as they had mine before sending me to Rio, and Ishway was now strapped to the chair with the metal crown adorning his bare scalp. As before, the long red cable emerged from the cap and ran down his side and behind the chair.

Unlike the Indian—unlike myself, if I'm being honest—Ishway wasn't pale. Though his bottom lip was split and bleeding, his right cheekbone purple and swollen with some abuse between the Handler's court and this sanctum of death, Ishway didn't sweat, or beg, or try to reason his way out. He'd lost on two counts—both by believing that Sage would let him reign, and that I wouldn't betray him given my inherent hatred of the Handler—and he knew it. He'd taken a massively ambitious gamble, and he wasn't about to apologize for that. So be it.

Had the two men at the cabin not displayed the map of Rocinha with the blast radius of a nuclear device, Ishway would already be dead, and Sage assuming the throne.

"Before you went to Brazil, David," the Handler said, "you saw a man die in this chair—Upraj Raza Sukhija, a man you knew as 'The Indian.'"

"Hard to forget," I allowed.

"During his process of recruiting you into the Outfit, you correctly surmised that he had an inside source within my Organization. The Indian passed off direct contact with his source to Ian, who was ecstatic about the arrangement. You knew this was wrong at an elemental level. On the surveillance recording of your conversation with Ian before you boarded your flight to Brazil, you warned him that the Indian was dead because his inside source 'burned' him."

"Thanks for the recap. I seem to recall that just fine on my own."

"David"—the Handler swung a hand toward Ishway's seated form—"meet the Indian's inside source. A man who was working for me all along, parceling out the misinformation I wanted the Indian to believe. Who enabled the capture of Ian, and led the Indian to this very throne—"

I interrupted, "And now Ishway will meet the same fate. I appreciate the poetic justice, so spare me the vengeful monologue. You want me to kill him for you."

"Not for me." The Handler gestured to the switch box with a long, Y-shaped handle canted toward the floor. "For yourself. You failed the test of loyalty when the Indian was in this throne. Now is your chance to prove yourself."

"I don't owe you a goddamn motherfucking thing. You have no idea what I've gone through while you've been holed up in your little palace here. We're not friends, and you'd better send me to South America because if I see you again I'll do everything in my power to slit your fucking throat."

Then I looked to Ishway, eyeing me levelly. He'd never heard anyone speak to the Handler in such a fashion, and he never would again. Whatever his cold eyes held, it wasn't disdain for me—rather, something that he kept inside, something that he would take into his smoking grave.

If I hadn't known the details of his planned transition to power, I would have respected him immensely. The sheer audacity of the assassination plot that he had undertaken with Sage at great personal risk had been masterfully choreographed for years leading up to this point.

Until I cast my vote with an ax.

Ishway said, "I make no apologies for what I've done. I'm a product, David, like you—of my desires and demons both."

I stared back at him. Ishway, the last living embodiment of Sage's horrible plan to incinerate thousands upon thousands of people in a split second. I thought of the favela girl who'd watched me hatefully in her kitchen, who would never forgive me for the danger I'd brought upon her regardless of whether I saved her from it in the end. Had I not used the ax on the command post occupants in the cabin, she'd be dead in the coming days.

"Relax, Ishway." I grinned, thinking this was like what I'd told Cong: a necessary execution. "I don't murder innocent people."

Ishway relaxed for a split-second reprieve, then suddenly tensed as he saw me reach for the switch.

Then he began screaming, his cry replaced by something far worse as I flipped the lever upward.

17

It was the same room that Sage had used to interrogate me, adorned with only a door, a table, and two empty chairs. One wall held a mirror that I knew blocked supervisors and video recording equipment on the other side. The entire room was surely wired for high-definition audio. It was surreal to be back here, now seven months removed from when I'd first entered, my left arm in a sling, to surrender myself to the Handler's scheme.

And then, to Sage's.

Two guards had led me in and directed me to take a seat, then said that I wouldn't have to wait long. Settling into the chair facing the open door, I watched the guards take up positions in the corners.

I scanned the ceiling—a gleaming black orb near each corner, filming every word and facial expression from multiple angles, streaming for analysis by the Handler's Intelligence Directorate. Hell, they'd probably allowed the meeting just to discover what Ian would tell me.

I wondered where he was at that moment. I'd last seen him on his knees, arms tied behind his back, the Handler's security team hoisting him up to take him to a cell. Most of all I remembered his vacant stare at the bitter end, when his best efforts and mine had come up grievously short.

And my last words to him before he was dragged away from me, spoken with conviction for his sake, although I'd had no idea if or how they could ever prove true.

I will get you out of this, Ian.

Ian suddenly walked into the room with a confident gait, his wiry form moving easily as he saw me and flashed a rakish grin. He looked healthy and fulfilled, eyes bright behind his thin glasses, very far removed from our last meeting in January.

A guard stopped him at the door and spoke to us both.

"No discussion about security measures for the One or this facility, or the deal's off. You've got five minutes. Then Ian will depart by plane, and you two will never meet again."

Ian sat in the chair across from me, folding his hands on the table.

I began, "It's good to see you, Ian."

He nodded. "I can never thank you enough for freeing me. Whatever you had to do to make this deal, I'm sure it took considerable sacrifice, and I'm very grateful for that."

I shrugged, grinning. "It took about as much effort as getting you stuck here in the first place. Though to hear the Intelligence Directorate sing your praises, I'm not sure you should leave. Elevated to targeting the executive network? Nice work, Ian."

Ian's eyes slid to a guard in the corner, then back to me. He rubbed his earlobe, looking nervous, pensive.

"Don't worry, Ian," I assured him. "You're free. The deal's been confirmed in front of the entire executive staff."

He replied uneasily, "It's not me I'm worried about. My life in the criminal realm is over, and I'll never look back after being given this chance. But you are about to enter a very dangerous war, David. Very dangerous."

"Not my first rodeo."

"But the war you're about to enter is...different," he warned. "From anything you've ever done."

Then his eyes assumed a very sober expression, his lips drawn tightly together as if he were about to say something upon which the fate of the universe rested.

"I would like to give you some advice. I need you to take it. Do you understand?"

Whatever Ian was about to say, he didn't want anyone but me to understand its import. He knew something that I didn't, and he wanted to relay it indirectly with the full knowledge that the Handler's people in the Intelligence Directorate were now dissecting our conversation.

But Ian was smarter than them. I'd never seen him look so stern—he'd figured out a way to tell me, and now the only point of failure was my ability to decipher his meaning.

"Ian," I said, "I understand that I'm about to enter a new war. Before I go, what advice do you have for me?"

Ian's entire demeanor shifted from nervous to forceful. Then he leaned toward me, folding his hands together as if in prayer, and opened his mouth to speak.

THE SUICIDE CARTEL: AMERICAN MERCENARY #5

David Rivers is no ordinary mercenary.

He's just been assigned command of a team in the international criminal war raging in South America.

But the Triple Frontier region is deadly. Narcos and terrorists rule its remote jungle, and David must lead his team into the heart of danger.

Getting in is easy. Getting out might be impossible.
When a high-risk recon mission turns deadly, David's team must fight for survival against overwhelming odds.

Desperate and on the run, they use everything at their disposal just to stay alive.

But getting out will require something more... and if David doesn't discover the truth behind his current mission, it will be his last.

Get your copy today at
severnriverbooks.com/series/the-american-mercenary

ACKNOWLEDGMENTS

As with my previous books, this fourth David Rivers installment has reminded me that I'm embarrassingly indebted to the many people who've invested their time, insight, and never-ending faith in this series.

My sister Julie once again scoured the initial drafts of this work several times over before they were fit for further scrutiny—as ever, I couldn't have proceeded without her.

A small crew of long-time readers next guided my hand in rewriting the manuscript—Derek, JT, and Codename: Duchess. Their feedback on structural elements of the story was vital to lifting it to the next level of development.

My beloved team of beta readers then imparted their wisdom and opinions, all of which contributed to the home stretch of book revisions.

Beta readers for this book are: Basque Bill, Bob Waterfield, Chet Manly, Dean Fukawa, Earl Kelley, Gabriella "Gabi" Rosetti, Gwendolyn Needham (RN, RM, Ba Health), Howard, J. Thoma, Jack Raburn, Janet, James Sexton (aka Hee Haw), Jeane Jackson, Jim Flagg, Joe Cunningham, Jon Suttle, M. Julien, MK, Ray Dennis, and Tim Abbott. Thank you all!

Spanier lent his medical expertise to advise me on the finer points of orthopedic surgery, ensuring accuracy for the descriptions of David's scarring and recovery from his gunshot wounds in Rio. He's since been hired as David Rivers's personal physician.

Howard Ryan offered an extensive forensic consult, without which Sage's plan to fake David's death would have failed at the outset—as an author, I owe him a debt of gratitude for ensuring that my protagonist lives to fight another day.

Cara Quinlan once again provided professional editing services that transformed the manuscript to a polished, publication-ready version. Combined with her extensive insight and suggestions throughout our month-long series of revisions for each book, she's become absolutely integral to this series.

Finally, my beautiful and long-suffering wife Amy deserves my thanks. Her support has not wavered in the slightest from the time I left my previous career to leap into the unknown as an author, right up to the conclusion of this fourth book. As a wife, mother, and personal story adviser, she's truly without equal.

ABOUT THE AUTHOR

Jason Kasper is the USA Today bestselling author of the Spider Heist, American Mercenary, and Shadow Strike thriller series. Before his writing career he served in the US Army, beginning as a Ranger private and ending as a Green Beret captain. Jason is a West Point graduate and a veteran of the Afghanistan and Iraq wars, and was an avid ultramarathon runner, skydiver, and BASE jumper, all of which inspire his fiction.

Sign up for Jason Kasper's reader list at
severnriverbooks.com/authors/jason-kasper

jasonkasper@severnriverbooks.com